PRAISE FOR JUDY PRESCOTT MARSHALL

With a blend of wit and charm, Judy Prescott Marshall is a modern-day Jane Austen.

— BEN REEDING

Stunning!

— LONGTIME READER

Once every so often the world hears a new voice. Judy Prescott Marshall is the person to whom that voice belongs.

— FELLOW AUTHOR

RHODE ISLAND RED

THE LIGHTHOUSE SERIES
BOOK 3

JUDY PRESCOTT MARSHALL

RHODE ISLAND RED

THE LIGHTHOUSE SERIES
BOOK 3

JUDY PRESCOTT MARSHALL

For David Wayne

1

On a cloudy and gray February morning everyone gathered at the First Baptist Church of Narragansett. Some, were hunched over, rubbing their hands together due to the bitter cold wind and quite possibly from the lack of clothing. David tried to greet every person as they entered the building. Aunt Emily offered to host lunch at a nice restaurant afterwards, but David insisted it be held at the inn in the large dining room. "Many won't attend out of fear they are not dressed appropriately." He kissed her on the cheek and thanked her for offering. "I'll make sure everyone knows they are welcome at the inn. In fact, I have a bus coming to take everyone to the luncheon."

As soon as David saw Grace, he openly cried. "I'm so sorry," he said as they hugged.

"My heart hurts knowing he was alone. Red, was my friend," she cried. "I will forever miss him."

"I wish I knew he had a heart condition," David said as he reached out to shake Steve's hand.

"I'm sorry for your loss," Steve said and then offered to take Grace's coat.

"Thank you for allowing me to read his eulogy," Grace said and then waved her hand out in front of them. "I think he would have liked this church. Thank you for taking care of all the arrangements." She shook her head in disbelief.

"Of course," David replied. "Grace, the doctor said Red experienced a massive, unexpected cardiac arrest, and the doctor promised me, Red hadn't felt much of anything. It was that quick and too overwhelming to be painful."

Grace buried her face in Steve's chest and cried. David nodded to Steve, shook his head and told Steve, "Grace was the only person able to get close to Red."

By ten o'clock the entire church was full. First David welcomed everyone for coming then he introduced the Pastor. "Welcome. Today, we gather and celebrate the life of Red. A man who seemed to have touched the hearts of many. I may not have known Red, however based on today's attendance, and listening to his friend, David Wayne, I am made to believe Red's kindness, and his unwavering faith in humanity goes far beyond what any of us can see." He looked out at the crowd, bowed his head in prayer and then read Psalm 34:18 from the Bible. "The Lord is close to the brokenhearted and saves those who are crushed in spirit." Pastor smiled at a man sitting in the front row. The man was obviously close to Red. He had tears in his eyes and every time he wiped them away, the man sitting next to him patted him on his leg. He smiled at the two men. "In this verse, God understands our feelings and helps us bear the burden of sorrow." He turned and looked over his shoulder at the photo of Red. (In the photo, Red appeared to be laughing at something Grace must have said to him. When Shelby heard the news of Red's passing, she framed the twenty-four by thirty-six-inch photo and hand delivered it to David.) Pastor glanced over at David. "As we say goodbye to Red, let us remember the beautiful memories he made within our hearts. May he rest in the loving arms of our Heavenly Father and may Red's memory be a blessing to all of us."

"Yes," David whispered.

Pastor held up the pamphlet David's assistant had printed for the occasion. "Inside your pamphlets you will find the words to "Go Rest High on That Mountain", you may sing along if you'd like." From the first lyric, pastor had everyone's attention. His voice was velvety and when he sang the words, "son your work on earth is done" men openly cried. David bowed his head in prayer.

Jude was touched by the moment and swore to help

David do whatever she could to help those in need. She reached over and cupped Aunt Emily's hands, giving them a squeeze, then she handed her a tissue. She too had tears in her eyes watching David. Next to the song lyrics was an invitation to the luncheon along with details explaining a bus would be outside waiting to take people to the inn for the celebration of life luncheon. When the song was over the pastor offered a final prayer followed by, "We are truly grateful for the privilege of having shared life with you. Amen."

Grace openly cried. Everyone heard Aunt Emily say, "Amen."

David wiped his eyes with the tissue, looked at the picture of Red, stood up and thanked the pastor for his kind words. "Thank you so much, your voice reached the heavens and left me breathless." He shook the pastor's hand before stepping up to the lectern. "I'd like to share a story with you." He looked at the photo again, pointed to it and then held his hand over his heart before saying, "It's true none of us knew Red's backstory or why he chose to be homeless, we were however, blessed to see his selflessness in action many times. From picking up garbage along our beaches to helping anyone in need. I, myself witnessed one of Red's kind acts. One day, I heard banging on my front door. It was Red. He was holding a woman in his arms. Red asked me to drive them to the hospital because she was having a brain aneurysm." David held his hand over his mouth, held back tears, swallowed the lump forming in his throat and continued, "Red was not only right about the woman, but thanks to his quick response he saved her life." David openly cried as he moved his hands from his mouth to his heart. "I'm sorry." The pastor handed David several tissues. "Thank you," David said and looked up. "On a different day, I was driving down the road and saw flames shooting out of windows in a two-story building. Red was standing on the sidewalk, he appeared to be in shock. He didn't respond or say anything, he just stood there, stoic. When I heard a woman call for help, I ran to the side of the building and saw her standing over a man covered in black soot. The woman told me she saw a man carry him out of the building. The man told the police his propane tank exploded, he was trapped behind a fallen bookshelf, he cried out for help and a man rushed in and saved him. That man was Red." David bowed his head, pointed to the ceiling and nodded before opening his eyes and saying, "Brooks and Dunn said it best—'Tell me there's more to life than a slow ride in a Hurst'. Red, you my friend will be forever in my heart and every time I see a set of footprints in the sand, I will think of you." He looked at Grace and when she nodded, he knew she was ready. "Grace would like to say a few words."

Steve stood up, extended his hand to Grace and then walked her up to the lectern. Steve and David both took their seats. Grace's eyes filled up fast as she glanced over at Red's picture. She too held her hand over her aching heart. She wiped her eyes, blew her nose and looked out at the crowd. A woman sitting in the back row gave Grace Goosebumps. Grace studied her for a long while before Steve asked her if she was okay. "Grace?" he whispered. "Sweetheart, are you okay?"

David turned around to see what Grace was looking at. Then Ava and Shelby looked back, followed by Aunt Emily.

Grace shook the thought off. "I'm sorry," she said and pointed to her stomach. "I'm pregnant and I think my baby fog got the best of me."

People chuckled. One woman nodded to Grace as she called out, "It's okay, honey. You take all the time you need."

Grace smiled at her and said, "Thank you." Then she continued, "It is true, Red was a selfless man who went through life helping others. He was chivalrous and a true gentleman. A lovely man who asked for nothing but offered so much." She looked at David and smiled. "I remember the night we met him. David and I were walking to my car when we saw a man next to the dumpster behind George's of Galilee. David thought Red was eating from the dumpster, but I saw Red pick the garbage up and toss it *in* the dumpster. David tried to give Red money for food, but Red refused David's generosity. Even when I begged him to take the money or I would lock David out of the house." Grace shook her head and offered a warm smile before continuing. "Red apologized to David for making him sleep under the stars." Grace watched as the woman in the back row wiped her eyes. Grace took a deep breath and said, "Red was a hero, a true-life saver. On a different day, I watched him save a little girl from drowning and in his humble self he simply walked away as if he did nothing at all." Grace wiped her tears away. "If not for Salty Brine Beach, I may not have ever met the most beautiful human being on this planet. Red was a gentle soul; a great listener and I am honored to call him my friend." Grace stepped down and when she saw the woman dressed in black turn to leave, Grace ran after her. They were both in the parking lot when Grace shouted, "Wait." She called out to her again, "Please, stop," Grace shouted as the woman opened the door to a black Mercedes. "I'm sorry, did you know Red?" Grace said as the woman closed her car door. Standing in front of the car, pregnant, with no coat, chills ran down Grace's spine when the woman made eye contact with her.

The woman opened her car door, got out and offered her coat to Grace. "You're shivering," she said as she wrapped the coat around Grace's shoulders and told her, "Yes. He was my father."

Behind them they could hear people coming out of the church. The bus driver pulled up to the front door. David announced for those who walked, to please join him for lunch in Red's honor.

Grace placed one hand on the hood of the car. The woman reached out and took hold of her. "Are you okay? Should I get someone for you?" Her voice was soft and she sounded just like Red.

"You." Grace swallowed a sob. "Are. His daughter?" she said and stood up straighter.

"Yes," the woman replied. "I'm Amelia."

2

Grace and Amelia watched as people boarded the bus. Grace waved a hand to Steve as he came out of the church. She handed Amelia back her coat and told her that Red was a good friend and she was sorry for her loss. "I'm so sorry," Grace said. "You." She smiled warmly at her. "You look just like him." Grace studied her red hair, her eyes and creamy white skin. Amelia's clothes were not of a homeless person, in fact, she was high class. From her heels to her Vera Wang coat, she breathed wealth. "Will you join us for lunch in honor of your father?" Grace reached out and touched her hand. "Please."

Amelia smiled up at Steve as he offered Grace her own coat, then she reached out to shake his hand and said, "I'm Amelia."

"I'm Steve, Grace's husband. It's nice to meet you."

"Steve, Amelia is Red's daughter."

Steve stuck his chin out. "Oh."

Amelia's eyes opened wide, knowing everyone was just as surprised at her attendance as she was to be there. She liked Grace and she was grateful for all the kind words spoken about her father. "I have some time before I have to get back. Yes, I will join you."

Grace put her coat on and said, "I can ride with you and show you where—"

Amelia looked at Steve. "If you don't mind."

"Not at all." Steve kissed Grace on the cheek and said he would see them in a few minutes.

Grace and Amelia got in the Mercedes. Amelia turned toward Grace. "My father truly was a good man. Both in life and in his death."

"He touched the lives of so many. Amelia, I don't understand," Grace said. "Why?"

"He didn't tell you about me, did he?"

"I'm sorry—"

Amelia placed her hand on Grace's. "It's okay. My father walked away for a reason. My heart bleeds, but if you knew my father, you would understand."

Grace swallowed the lump forming in her throat. "Why was he homeless?" She wiped away a tear with the back of her hand. "He was intelligent and obviously well educated."

Amelia offered a gentle smile. "Everything he ever learned was from a textbook. My father had no formal education. He learned his craft by reading books on the subject. I remember the day he brought home an entire set of encyclopedias; my mother asked him where he had gotten the books and what on earth did he intend on doing with them. He told her he rescued them from a dumpster and he planned on reading them." She looked at Grace and smiled. "My father read the entire set of Britannica Encyclopedia to me and my brother." Then she looked out and saw the last car leave the parking lot. "He was the best carpenter in Connecticut."

"Connecticut?" Grace looked at her. "I'm from Connecticut." She sucked in a breath. In a low and cautious voice, she asked, "Do you think he had a nervous breakdown?"

"Perhaps," Amelia offered. "We can only speculate as to how he felt after the accident." When it started getting cold, she turned the ignition on along with the seat warmers. "I wasn't going to come out of fear I would have to go back to that day, now I am thinking—"

"Amelia—"

"It's okay. It might be a good way for me to finally understand where my father was all this time. I had no idea he was living life as a homeless man until a colleague called me and said she found my father."

Grace could feel herself heating up with anticipation of Amelia's story, never mind her derriere was on fire. When she unbuttoned her coat, Amelia turned down the heat. "Thank you," Grace said. "I thought I was having a hot flash for a minute there and they both laughed.

Amelia looked out at the empty parking lot and asked if they should get going. "Maybe, we should head over."

"I'd like to hear what happened *if* that's okay with you."

Silence. Then Amelia smiled at Grace and said, "It wasn't his fault. It truly was an accident."

Grace took a deep breath and nodded. "I'm just trying to understand why such a wonderful man chose the life he did."

"I'm sure," she replied and lowered the seat warmer even more. "I was moving to New York that day. We all ate breakfast at the kitchen counter. My father lit a fire in the kitchen fireplace for me. My mother always tried to get me to eat at the table, but I loved the warmth on my back while eating." Tears streamed down her face remembering. "If my father saw me doing my home-work at the counter, he would kiss me on the back of my head and proceed to light a fire for me. Even if it was eighty degrees outside, he knew how much I loved sitting by the fire. My parents were so happy that morn-ing. My little brother was about to enter the twelve grade and he too wanted to work in the medical profes-sion." She took a deep breath. "After breakfast, they drove me to Columbia University. I knew my father was having a hard time leaving me, when he insisted, we all go out for dinner in Manhattan." She paused for a moment. "It was past midnight when they returned home. I'm sure they were exhausted. Especially my parents, who were usually in bed by nine." Silence.

Grace studied Amelia's face; she felt bad, horrible in fact. "I can't imagine what you're going through right now."

Amelia blew out a long breath. "We were all running around, packing the car with my personal belongings, making sure I didn't leave anything behind, when my mother told my father we had better get going because traffic into the city on a Sunday was not going to be pleasant. I watched my father set the bucket of ashes from the fireplace out on the back porch. I didn't think anything of it. Sometime during the night, the wind must have kicked up the ambers and the furniture caught on fire. Everyone was sleeping on the third floor. By the time the smoke alarm had gone off, it was too late. The entire kitchen below was gone. The staircase was engulfed. The fireman said my father must have jumped out a window, because when they arrived, he was standing below yelling for my mother and brother to jump." Tears streamed down both of their faces.

"I'm so sorry," Grace said and then reached in her pocket for a handful of tissues.

Amelia blew out another long breath. "I'm sorry. That was ten years ago and yet it feels like it was yesterday."

"Amelia, you don't have to say anymore. I'm so sorry I upset you. I never meant to bring you more pain. I'm sure you have endured your share and now to lose your father."

Amelia looked at Grace. "How long did you know my father?"

"Four years, but I only saw him from time to time. If I was lucky, I would see him walking along the beach." She shook her head. "He was forever picking up other people's trash." She wiped her nose. "I had lunch with him one time. That's when I knew there was something deeper to be discovered, but I treasured our friendship more than my curiosity to know why he chose to be homeless."

"No one knew where he disappeared to, but we all understood. He loved my mother so much. He fell in love with her in the first grade, vowed to take care of her till the day he died. I remember watching her as she stood in the kitchen every night waiting for him to come home from work. She would hand him a snack knowing he worked all day, forgetting to stop and eat because he was such a perfectionist. We used to tell him he had OCD because he was such a neat freak." She glanced at the church steeple, looked up at the sky and thought, *I love you Dad and I miss you so much.* "I was in my biology class when they told me about the fire. My father wasn't answering my calls. I assumed his phone burned in the fire. I called a friend to come and get me. When we got to the house, everything was gone, even my father. A week later, I returned to college. I was in my dorm room when I received a call from my parent's attorney. He told me my father was devastated and that he had left everything to me, even the insurance money." She blew out a breath. "My father was a self-made millionaire. He could have chosen to live like one, but instead he became a homeless man to punish himself." She reached over and took Grace's hand in her own. "Thank you for being such a good friend to my father. I am sure he valued your friendship. I was glad to hear he still wore his donor bracelet. Did they tell you he donated his organs?"

Grace was sobbing when she shook her head and whispered, "No."

"The hospital administrator told me Mr. Wayne paid for everything."

Grace wiped away her tears, blew her nose and said, "I'm not surprised; he's a very generous person. He respected your father. The first night we met your father, David gave him his business card and told him if he ever needed anything at all to call him." Grace inhaled. Wiped another tear from her eye. "We were attending a friend's wedding when David received the call from the hospital. Thank God, your father kept David's card all this time."

"I can't believe he died on Valentine's Day," Amelia said. "David sounds like a good person."

"He's the salt of the earth. He's building an entire community for the homeless. He begged me to get your father to move there. But Red wouldn't have it. He said he chose to be homeless for a reason. Now I know the burden he carried. It's just sad. I wish David and I knew what Red was going through. Amelia, you should meet David." She tapped her on her arm. "I won't say a word to anyone about the fire if you don't want me to."

"Maybe, my father's story will inspire someone to reach out to their own family. I'm afraid there may be a lot of good people taking the same road my father took and believe me they don't have to. It breaks my heart to think he felt so guilty that he stopped living life. He was such a good carpenter; he could build anything. Our home may have been over two-hundred years old, but it was filled with all the modern amenities. If I *had* found him, I would have told him it was not his fault. It was an accident. I would have liked to have him there for me, especially when I graduated."

Grace thought for a second. "Knowing the love in your father's heart, I'm sure he was right there. Maybe, he sat in the back row and you didn't see him."

Amelia leaned over and hugged Grace. "Thank you for saying that." Then she put the car in drive. "Shall we go?"

Grace nodded. "Go left out of the parking lot," she said and then told her the address. "It's not far. David rebuilt the inn to help save the fishing industry."

"Seriously?" Amelia blew out a breath. "Wow, he's a great man." She snapped her neck as she looked at Grace. "Thank goodness, my roommate from Columbia works at the hospital morgue. She told me David's business card was the only thing in my father's pocket. She said as soon as she saw my father, she knew it was him." Amelia rubbed her forehead with her fingertips. "I'm so glad I kept a photo of my parents on my nightstand, otherwise who knows how this all would have ended."

A loud breath escaped Grace, her stomach dived and chills ran down her spine at the thought. "That would have been awful." Then she pointed to the inn. "We're here."

Amelia parked the car at the end of the parking lot, got out and laced her arm through Grace's as they entered the inn. "Maybe God brought us together for a reason."

3

The room was overflowing with people, staffers and yes, the homeless. Steve informed everyone where Grace was and whom she was with. David was shocked by the news of Red having a child and never mentioning her to anyone. Aunt Emily reminded him that it was not his place to judge. Jude said that if David knew, perhaps he could have helped Red find his daughter. "Maybe if David knew, he could have done something to help Red," she said as Grace walked in with Amelia. Jude saw David's eyes open wide. She asked him if he was okay. "You look like you just saw a ghost. Are you okay?"

"She's older than I expected." David said and then looked into Amelia's eyes. "She's Red's daughter all right."

Jude didn't know what to expect. Perhaps David was

expecting Grace to walk in with a child and not a knock-down gorgeous red head.

Grace introduced Amelia to David, Jude and to Aunt Emily. Of course, Amelia knew exactly whom Emily was. "I have all of your cookbooks," Amelia said to her as she accepted a glass of sparkling water from a server. "Thank you."

Aunt Emily gave Amelia a warm hug. "I'm so sorry for your loss."

"Thank you." Then she turned toward David and said, "I can't thank you enough for being an exceptional friend to my father." When she reached up to give him a hug, David bent down and held her in his arms for a moment.

They both had tears in their eyes when they heard Aunt Emily say, "God's plans are not always clear. Perhaps Red's mission was to bring everyone together for something much bigger."

David leaned back and told Amelia he was delighted to meet her.

She tapped his hand and said, "I'm so glad I came." Her green eyes sparkled as she wiped away a tear.

Amelia spent the rest of the afternoon listening to people tell their own personal stories about her father. A woman wearing tattered clothing said Red stood up for her when another man tried taking a coat from her. A man spoke up and said, "Red was always kind to me. When my sugar was low, he would sit next to me until I felt strong enough to get up again. One day, I saw Red at the beach. He was resting along the water's edge with no shoes on his feet. The tides drifted in and out, but he didn't care. I asked him where his shoes were. He said he gave them to the shoemaker's son and we both laughed. The following week, I saw a young boy wearing Red's shoes."

Tears filled Amelia's eyes hearing all the wonderful stories and memories of her father. As much as she wanted to stand up and share what a loving father he was, she was drained. When Grace offered to get her a slice of cake, Amelia told her she needed to get back to the hospital. "I'm on call tonight."

"Are you a doctor?" Grace asked.

"No, I'm an anesthesiologist at Northwell Health in Bay Shore," she replied. "I'm so glad our paths crossed. Promise me you will stay in touch." She handed Grace several business cards. "Please give David my card and thank you both for today." She looked around the room. "If you didn't chase me like a mad woman, I would have missed this." Then she hugged Grace.

Grace handed Amelia her own business card. "If you need anything at all... please call me. I'm a good listener. Amelia, you made today more bearable, understand-able. I am so glad you shared your story with me." She looked into her eyes. "You have your father's heart. Your love for him shines and the fact that you saw his home-lessness as a way for him to heal... is so heartwarming."

Amelia winked at Grace. "You take care of yourself and keep me posted on David's progress with the shelter."

Grace chuckled. "Shhhh, it's not a shelter. It's a living community." Grace and Amelia held each other for a long poignant moment. Then Grace drew away and cradled Amelia's face in her hands. "Thank you for coming." Offering a coy smile as she wiped a single tear from Amelia's cheek.

Amelia's smile was delicate almost sweet when she nodded. "You're welcome." She put her coat on and waved goodbye as she walked out of the dining room. Grace was so grateful to have met her. When she turned back around and saw Steve standing near the dessert table. She walked up to him and asked if she could have a hug. "Saying goodbye to Amelia was like saying farewell to Red. Forever."

Steve held her in his arms. "It's funny how things turned out." Then he looked into her eyes. "How did you know she was his daughter?"

Grace shook her head. "I didn't. She stood out from everyone else and when she cried, I knew I had to find out who she was."

"So, you ran after her." He tilted his head and tapped her on her nose. "No more running in high heels."

As people started to head toward the door, David reminded them about the new living facility. He was so proud of his chef and new innkeeper for taking the time to put together goody bags with an invitation to visit the facility.

"Thank you," one woman said to Charlie as she held up her bag. "When I eat the cookie tonight, I will think of Red. He loved cookies."

Another woman told Charlie she liked the smell of the shampoo. When Charlie saw a man take two bags, he quietly handed him three more. The man simply nodded as he accepted them. "A few people couldn't make it. Their legs never would have made the trek."

David stepped in closer, held out his hand and thanked him for thinking about his friends. "I'm sorry I didn't provide a ride to the church." David didn't care the man's coat was dirty. The only thing he saw was a kind and thoughtful heart. He tapped him on his shoulder twice telling him, "I'll work on transportation. Thank you for thinking of the others."

The inn's chef put her hand on Charlie's back, winked at him and whispered, "We should all have his heart and his mindset."

David said goodbye to Grace and Steve and thanked them for coming. He asked Shelby and Ava if they could stay a minute longer. "Shelby, thank you for the picture. I'd like to keep it and hang it somewhere at the new place."

"If you want, I have photos from today," she said as she held her camera up.

"Let me think about it," he replied and put his hand on Ava's shoulder. "I have a proposition for you."

Ava smiled as she offered David a quick response, "You do?"

He handed her an envelope. Inside was a blank check. "Will you design a line of clothing for the men and women that anyone can wear? By that I mean, anyone from a small frame individual to an extra-large person."

Ava looked at him. "I know exactly what you need." She looked at Shelby. "Wrap coats with drawstrings for the ladies and jackets with inserts for the men."

"Inserts?" David asked.

"Yes," Ava said and showed him what she was talking about. She drew an example on a napkin. "If the man is a small, he can remove anywhere from one to three side panels."

Shelby used her hand to show him what Ava was talking about. "Imagine a zipper here, here and here." Ava giggled as Shelby tickled her side.

"Ahh, yes. Perfect. And how about pants, hats, gloves?" he said.

"David, I'm on it," Ava replied. "Let me call my manufacture and I'll get back to you by next week. What's my budget?"

David pointed to the envelope. "Whatever it takes."

Over the next few weeks, David was busy trying to

complete the construction. Thankfully, March rolled in with temperatures in the high fifties. Jude was in New York for the launch of her new book and Aunt Emily was spending the weekend in Florida in The Villages at her friend Geraldine's new sunny house. David took the time to meet with his own team. He was amazed at the progress. The grocery store, drug store and most of the commercial buildings were in place. When he arrived at the living facility, his assistant was busy in the model home showing two people the layout. "Hi," she said as David entered the makeshift office set up in the living room.

"Everything looks great," he said and held his hand out to the two men.

"Tom, Andy, this is—"

"Mr. Wayne," the men said in perfect unison.

"It's nice to meet you. Thank you for doing this," the man wearing a Vietnam Era 1960 to 1975 Veteran hat said.

Both men were wearing fatigue field jackets. David shook their hands. "Thank you both for your service and dedication to our country. Honestly, you are my inspiration and you're both heroes in my eyes."

What his assistant didn't tell him was... she allowed them to use the shower and she gave them both new underwear and socks prior to meeting David. Faith winked at the men as she told David she was trying to tell them they did not have to pay anything to live there. "They both served our country and both Andy and

Tom are on disability. I assured them they qualified for the program and I would love to see them each take a home near the community center because the swimming pool would be wonderful for their physical therapy." Then she handed Andy his cane. When he stepped closer to her, David noticed he had to hold onto the wall.

"I'd listen to her if I were you." Then David pointed to the map on the wall. "These two units are available and they are right next to each other. What do you say?"

Tom put his hand out, palm up. "I only make six-hundred dollars a month."

David took hold of his hand, tapped it twice. "And every cent of that money is yours to spend on whatever you need. All the amenities are included, including your utilities. I won't ask you for one penny. In fact, I just purchased a wheelchair van for transportation to and from doctor appointments or wherever you all need to go."

"It's all free?" Faith said and then put her arm around Andy. "Come on, I'll show you your new home."

Andy wiped his eye before saying, "I hated the shelter." Then he laced is arm through Faith's. "I feel like I am in a dream."

"Wait until you climb into bed." She winked at David. "The bedding arrived yesterday." Then she looked at the men and said, "Yes, your homes will be move in ready. From cotton to flannel sheets for a warm and cozy cold night's sleep to towels, dishes, pans and utensils. We've got you."

David reminded them about the medical center and the food pantry on site. "I'll also be giving every person a prepaid store card to use at the grocery store so you can buy whatever you want."

"Steak? I can buy a steak. I haven't eaten a good steak in years," Andy said.

"Whatever you want," Faith said as she glanced back at David knowing the prepaid card was something new.

When David raised his eyebrows at her and then his shoulders, she winked at him as if to say I'm on it, "Great idea, Boss." and gave him a thumbs up.

As they approached the first home, David told them, "Our country owes you so much. This is just the beginning." David held the door open for them. "Welcome to your new home."

4

Aunt Emily was in the garden feeling concerned hearing the news about Jude not returning from New York for an extended amount of time. She had high hopes for Jude and David. She picked the last stigmas from the saffron crocus to dry and later use in her finer recipes. She walked into the kitchen, set the basket on the counter, removed her garden gloves and spread the stigmas on a kitchen towel to dry and later jar. As much as she wanted to go and see David in person, she worried about overstepping her boundaries. When she picked up her cellphone and saw he had left her a voicemail, she raised her hand and said, "Thank you." After listening to his message, she decided to call him.

David picked up on the first ring. "Hello—"

"David, I received your message. Of course you can

use my name as a reference. I'm so glad you're seeking backers for the project. I would be happy to make a few calls on your behalf. I can call my dear friend at PepsiCo. I also have a contact at Kimberly-Clark and at Ford," she said looking around. "Oh, wait. I just know Tyson Foods will want to be included once I tell them about the project."

"Great," he replied and scratched his brow. "I'm worried about the future. I don't want people to say yes to a one-time delivery, I'm hoping they sign up for the long haul."

"Then type up a contract and make them commit to a ten-, twenty- or a fifty-year plan. You know what? Why don't you let me speak to your attorney Allan, between the two of us we'll structure a deal they can't say no to? We'll offer them free publicity and—"

"I love you," he said and shook his head. "Where would I be without you? Thank you. I'll call Allan and let him know to expect your call."

She took a deep breath and cocked her head to the side. "David, can I ask you what you are planning to do about Jude?"

David chuckled. "What would you like for me to do with her? No, wait. Don't answer that. Aunt Emily—"

"Does it bother you that she is not back from New York yet?"

"Aunt Emily, Jude went back for the week because her novel launches this week and thanks to you, she hit the New York Times bestseller list so she has her hands full at the moment."

"How wonderful. I'm so glad I introduced her to my street team. Good for her. When is she coming back?"

"You're not going to let it go, are you?" He shrugged unsure how else to respond.

"I'd like to see you settle down and Jude is a lovely woman. She's perfect for you," she told him as she swatted a fly away.

Sunlight streamed in, reminding David it was time to head over to the construction site. "I would love to settle down. Believe me, I—" he closed his eyes allowing the sun to warm his senses.

"What sweetheart?" she said and sat down, trying to make herself comfortable.

"I like Jude. Maybe a little too much. I'm not interested in a long-distance relationship thou."

She brushed her hand along the armchair's side, smiled and said, "David, Ina and Jeffrey have a successful marriage for more than fifty years."

David knew exactly who she was referring to, she's mentioned Ina Garten several times over the years. They did have a great marriage. "I don't want a weekend bride. I'd like to share my life with someone full time. Aunt Emily, she's out there and one day I will find her."

"But, not Jude?"

"I'm sorry," he said and had to hang the phone up. "I

need to get going. Thank you for helping me find backers for the project."

"Bye, David." She disconnected the call feeling angry. She knew if Jude and David were to have a relationship, she would have to do more to convince Jude to move to Point Judith. "Hello, Geraldine. How are you dear?"

"I'm great. How are you these days?"

"We need to talk," Aunt Emily said as she got up and checked her schedule for the next week. "Can you meet me in Manhattan on Wednesday?"

"I don't see why not. Where would you like to meet?" Geraldine asked.

"Let's meet at Blank Street Coffee at nine, I'll buy you breakfast and fill you in on my new idea. I may have an investment for the two of us to go in on."

Geraldine wrote down the date and time in her calendar and replied, "I just love discovering hidden gems. I look forward to hearing all about your idea."

They disconnected the call and both women clapped their hands. Aunt Emily was proud of herself for even thinking about buying Jude out. Geraldine respected Aunt Emily enough to trust her idea and go along with whatever plan she may have hidden up her sleeve.

5

David received a thank you card along with a check for one-hundred-thousand dollars from Amelia. The scented paper had a gold seal marked Grasse, France. David inhaled the delicate rose fragrance and smiled. "She's perfect, just like you." Then he glanced over at Red's picture. "I should call her, right?" He reached for his cellphone, poured himself a bourbon and took it out to the back deck. He set the glass down on the table and moved closer to the railing. The sun was going down and the fireball in the sky meant hotter days were rolling in. No one was in sight. The air was salty as it should be and the temperature was perfect for strolling down the beach. When he turned around his cellphone chimed. He picked it up, looked at it and saw a message from Vista Print to order new business cards. A chill ran down his arms thinking about the day he gave his card to Red. He picked up his glass and took a sip before dialing her number.

She picked up on the first ring. "Hi, David."

"Amelia, thank you for your contribution. It means the world to me and to the residents."

"You're welcome," she replied, got up and closed the door to her office. When she sat back down at her desk, she looked at the photo of her parents and smiled. "I called and spoke to Faith, she's very good. In fact, she's so thorough, I wanted to tour the entire community."

"Thank you for saying that. I'll be sure to let her know she's doing a good job. I hope she invited you to the grand opening?"

"She did and I wouldn't miss it. One more thing, a few of my colleagues said they too would like to donate to the community. Dr. Jeffries has a weekend home in Newport, he said he could do house calls whenever he is in Rhode Island."

"That's wonderful," David said. "You have no idea what this means to me."

"David, you were good to my father and I appreciate that. I wish you could have met him on different terms. He was such a good builder and I am sure he would have loved to be a part of your project."

"Did he know he had a heart condition?" David asked wishing he had gotten closer to Red.

"No, not that I am aware of. Believe me, if my mother

knew he had a problem she would have made him go to the doctor. David, I—"

He waited for her to continue. When he heard her cry, he said, "I'm here for you. You can tell me anytime you need to talk or cry."

"Thank you for everything," she replied. "I promise, I'll see you soon."

"Amelia," he said in a low bass voice. "Please say you'll call me—"

"I think he died of a broken heart," she cried.

David heard what sounded like a pager going off. "I agree," he said sounding choked up.

After an incredibly long pause, she said, "I have to go."

"Take care, I look forward to meeting you again," he said and emptied his shot glass.

Amelia wiped her eyes, took a deep breath and took her pager out of her pocket. "David... I am glad I had a chance to visit Point Judith. It's beautiful and I can see why my father chose to live there, it has a wonderful sense of belonging," she quietly said. "I'm sorry I need to go. Bye for now."

"Bye, Amelia."

Amelia answered her page and made her way to the third-floor operating room. At nine o'clock that evening, Amelia sat quietly in her office thinking about her father, wondering if he did attend her graduation ceremony. She pulled out the album and looked at the pictures hoping to see her father. She didn't see him in the photo when she received her diploma, but there he was standing in the back row right before everyone tossed their caps in the air. Amelia held the photo close to her heart and cried. A moment later, she got up and went home. Too tired to cook, she reached for a banana and smiled. "I know. I'm just like him. Sorry, Mom." Then she climbed into bed. The next morning, she woke from a dream. She dreamt she was married to David Wayne and they were living in Rhode Island. She tossed the covers back, stood up and smoothed her Cami T—shirt down to her panty line. She looked at her reflection in the mirror and said, "Seriously, Dad?" After Amelia drank her coffee, she did yoga, showered and headed back to the hospital. She was driving down the Long Island Expressway when it hit her—her father purposely kept David's card so they would meet.

David immediately called Faith to give her the news of Dr. Jeffries and to thank her for doing a good job. "I spoke to Amelia and she was singing your praises."

"Aww, thank you. Seriously, I love my job. Did she tell you she's coming to the grand opening and that she has a list of doctors willing to donate money to ensure the program is a success?"

"She mentioned it," he said honestly with a slight grin.

"I sent her a follow up email so she can pass it along to everyone interested."

David went to say something, but Faith interrupted him. "I—"

"Wait, I wanted to surprise you, but I might as well tell you now. Three women signed up today. They're all—"

In spite of the buzz of excitement, David heard her crying.

"Faith, are you okay?"

"David, all three women are widows, collecting pennies from social security. One woman has terrible restless leg syndrome and needs to work at the grocery store part-time just to make enough money to buy food," Faith cried even harder. "I'm sorry, I just hate—"

"I know and that's why we are going to make sure they don't suffer any longer," he said and then told her he would see her in an hour. "Can I bring you anything?'" he asked.

Faith wiped her eyes, nose and said, "No thank you." She looked out the window and saw John coming up the sidewalk. "John's here. Wait until you see the garden they put in and the cabinets in the community center's kitchen. They're gorgeous."

David chuckled. "Okay, tell John I'm on my way. If he has a problem, call me back."

"Sounds good, bye." Then she waved to John. "I just spoke to David, he's on his way."

"Were you crying?"

"I'm fine. I just get a little emotional seeing so many

people suffering." She wiped her eyes and tossed the tissues in the garbage.

John informed her the last of the homes were being delivered next week. "Apparently, he has an entire convoy coming. I thought we could come up with an idea to surprise David so he was here to see it."

Faith looked at the map. "That's over a hundred homes."

"I know," John replied. "Cool, right?"

"Very cool." She stood up and told John she had an idea how to make sure David was there to see the houses rolling in. "I'll take care of it."

"Everyone I talk to says this place is amazing and what he's doing is—"

Faith smiled fondly. "Wonderful, right?"

"Yeah," he said and closed the office door behind him.

As soon as David climbed into the Tahoe, his cell-phone rang. He answered her call. "Hey, you. How's the book launch going?"

"Busy, I can't believe how exciting and busy I have been. I cried when I saw my new book cover. I can't believe I reached number one. I haven't slept since I arrived. We have been celebrating nonstop. We had dinner at Wolfgang's last night and tonight we're going to Per Se, do you know how long the waiting list is to get in that place? A year," she said.

"I'm happy for you," he replied. "How'd you managed that reservation?"

"My new editor has his own table. He's such a pantser, but I like him, he keeps me on my toes."

"Huh, you went dancing?" David asked wondering if her new editor was behind the extended stay.

"No," Jude said. "I said pantser, not dancer. He goes by the seat of his pants. He makes me think twice about every word. He's the best editor I have ever worked with. You would like him, he's a younger version of you. Okay, I need to go. I'm meeting with Aunt Emily's publicist in ten minutes."

"Enjoy your day, I'll see you soon," David said, ended the call and put the vehicle in drive.

6

The rain finally stopped and the sun was shining over Manhattan. Jude has not sleep since she arrived home, she was too excited about her book tour, especially the part where she gets to meet new readers. Aunt Emily's publicist made all the arrangements from hitting a new line of book stores across America to obtaining Saks Fifth Avenue to sponsor her entire wardrobe for the tour. Jude loved all of the suits, they were sassy, and short. Every outfit matched the cover of her book. Her favorite suit was the one with the blue hydrangeas on it by Rickie Freeman for Teri Jon, from the Saks Folio Collection. For the final stop she planned on wearing the short shirt dress with sequins and fringe that moved as she walked. When Jude heard there was going to be over a thousand women in attendance and she only had ten hours to sign the books, she almost fainted.

Friday she flies out to California and from there she'll hit seven book stores, three libraries, ending the book tour at The Bergen Performing Arts Center in New Jersey where she will sign even more books and be interviewed by the queen of beach reads herself, Elin Hildebrand. She wants to interview Jude for her new podcast, Friends and Fiction. Jude's new publicist even booked Jude a slot on The Kelly Clarkson Show the first week in April. Her heart was still racing from hitting number one right before launch week. She had so much to look forward to from her book signings to seeing her new book cover graced with the words: New York Times Bestseller. Just as exciting, Barnes and Noble was offering an exclusive edition with sprayed edges and a map of the city along with a matching bookmark, and stickers.

The surprises just keep coming. At ten o'clock last night her publicist informed her they were going on a secret mission to Barnes and Noble in Union Square. Jude didn't know what she was up to but it sounded like fun. She laughed when the publicist told her not get dressed until she arrived. Jude jumped in the shower, blew her hair out and put on her lipstick. At eight-thirty her doorman alerted her of an arrival. Jude quickly put on a robe and opened the door.

"Morning," her publicist said as she handed her a double breasted navy blazer. "I think you should wear this with your thigh high boots."

Jude laughed. "No pants?"

"Nope. It will be flirtatious like Alex in the story. I want to get a lot of pictures of you walking in the city. Standing outside the bookstore and secretly signing books." She held up her index finger and then read a text message. "Congratulations! You have a sold out crowd at the Performing Arts Center."

"Seriously?" Jude replied as she accepted the blazer.

"Oh, yeah. All thirteen-hundred seats are sold." She pointed to the blazer and said, "Come on, let's go and by the way you look like hell." She reached in her bag and took out her foundation La Maison Valmont. "You need a little more than lipstick and mascara this morning. Have you even slept a wink?"

Jude offered a gentle smile. "I'm too excited." Then she smelled the bottle. "It smells like money."

"It's Sea Bliss and you're worth it. Today is a special day. I'm going to take a lot of pictures of you, starting right now." She pointed to the balcony. "Go stand out there and hold your hands up to the sky, because baby this city is yours and you are taking it by storm."

Jude did exactly as she was told. The one thing Aunt Emily told her was, "If you want to hit number you'll have to do everything my team tells you to do."

The women walked outside and strolled down the

streets of Manhattan laughing, talking and making plans for future novels. Jude stopped before crossing the road and asked, "Are we walking the entire way?"

"It's only three miles and yes." Then she motioned for Jude to cross the street. "Smile." As she snapped a few more pictures.

Jude stood outside the tall building and a breath escaped her as she looked up at the four-story store featuring the largest selection of books in the US. Jude stepped inside and immediately looked around. "Wow."

They made their way to the women's fiction section and saw a roundtable filled with Jude's new release. They both started laughing when one of the clerks asked what they were doing. Then she recognized Jude and asked if she could take a picture with her. From that moment on the camera never stops. Out in the street they saw a woman reading Jude's book near a food truck.

"I have one more surprise for you," the publicist said as she laced her arm through Jude's.

When Jude saw the ten by six foot mock of her book outside her publisher's building, she cried. "I thought getting the call I hit number was amazing. This is incredible." She turned and hugged everyone as they welcomed her inside the lobby.

There Jude signed even more books. Those books were for book clubs throughout the United States. Jude smiled as people walked past. Every now and then the publicist would ask a few women to come inside for a photo with Jude sitting behind the signing table.

At five-thirty, Jude signed more books than she could count and smiled for more cameras than a bride on wedding day. "I'm starving," she proclaimed.

"Me too. My treat. Let's go to Mission Ceviche. It's right around the corner."

They split an order of Roll Acevichado—Shrimp Tempura, Mahi Mahi tartare on thinly sliced avocado with ponzu gel. Jude ordered the risotto with roasted shrimp and her publicist ordered her favorite—octopus anticuchero.

"A toast, to one of my new favorite fiction writers."

They clicked glasses, then the publicist told Jude to hold her cocktail up again so she could take a picture with the big blue sparkling fish in the background. "Nice, this one is going on Instagram right now. Oh, by the way. Emily asked me when you were returning to Point Judith."

Jude inhaled, looked around the restaurant and smiled. "I still have ten days left on my tour and I'm thinking I may stay in the city until I do the Kelly Clarkson Show the first week in April." But then Jude thought about David. If she did stay in the city until the fifth of April that would mean she would only return to Point Judith for three weeks before she returned to Manhattan for good. There dinner arrived and Jude was still thinking about David. She moved a shrimp, flipped another one over before taking her first bite. Jude set her fork down. "I'm in trouble."

Her publicist also set her fork down, wiped the corners of her mouth and took a sip of her water. "Care to share." She raised her eyebrows, tilted her head, reached out and touched Jude's hand. "There isn't anything I can't handle. If you're not comfortable with something I need to know so I can figure out a way to fix it."

Jude offered a crimson smile. "I think I'm falling in love."

The publicist took back her hand and returned Jude's smile.

"The thought of me going back to Rhode Island and having to say goodbye to David seems unbearable. I can't believe I am about to say this but I'm in love with him."

"That's a good thing. Right?" She shook her head. "Wait. David? Like Emily's nephew, David?"

Jude nodded.

"Wow, I didn't see that one coming. I met him at Emily's one time. He's gorgeous." She swallowed the mounting saliva and took a sip of her cocktail, then she emptied it entirely. "I had no idea the two of you were even seeing each other." She waved to their server to bring two more drinks. "So that means you're moving to Rhode Island?"

"No," Jude protested. "My life is here in the city, I

need to be here. It's in my blood. How can I be a writer and—"

"What?" she asked.

"Live anywhere else. I know that sounds stupid, but this is all I know. Everyone is here in the city. I don't want to live anywhere else, but I want him in my life."

"You can still be with David and keep your apartment in the city for when you have meetings and need to write." She thanked the waiter for bringing their drinks, took a sip and said, "There's nothing saying you can't have both. You can live in the city while you're writing and go see David after you hand your manuscript to your editor. I know a lot of writers that live."

"I don't want a long distance relationship." Jude shrugged her shoulders. "If I'm missing him now and I've only been gone for a few days, how on earth will I survive writing sprints?" Jude thought about her book tour, traveling alone and then she thought about David and how he made her feel during their trip to Alaska. "I don't want to do this alone," she whispered to herself. Then she picked up her fork and ate everything on her plate. "That was so good. I am never going to fit into that sequence dress."

Her publicist was quiet. Every now and then Jude saw her tapping her fingers on the table and she wondered if she was thinking about the rest of the tour or Jude sharing the news of Emily's nephew.

"Are you upset that I added a few more book stores to the end of the tour?"

"No," Jude replied and sipped her water remembering what Aunt Emily told her. "Believe me, I know it was all part of the plan. I wanted to hit number. Aunt Emily warned me it was a lot of work." Jude laughed out loud. "She actually told me to do whatever you said or forget about hitting number one."

"Hell yeah!" She held up her water glass. "Number one Baby!" Then she set her glass down. "Your more important than a number to me, so if you ever feel like I am asking you to do something or I'm taking you away from your loved ones for too long of a period of time, let me know, because I can always break up the tour dates."

Jude thought about how much she was paying her. Aunt Emily assured Jude the publicist was worth every dime. At first, Jude didn't think she was even human, she was so focused and demanding, but now she seems softer and caring. "Thank you for saying that."

"Jude, I can schedule events throughout the year. Everyone is into pre-launch campaigns these days. You don't have to go away for three straight weeks."

Jude offered a wry grin. "I want both. I want to write and I want him in my life."

Their server brought the check over to the table. Jude watched the publicist add a twenty-five percent tip to the bill before she set her Discover card in the billfold. "I'm lucky," she said adding, "I'm married to a workaholic. We both have long days, but we also take time to schedule long vacations together." She smiled as she stood up. "You're a smart woman you'll figure it out." She put her hand on Jude's shoulder. "The heart knows when it's in love."

7

It was a classic springtime day in New York, the streets were filled with blooming flowers, comfortable weather, and vibrant life popping up everywhere. Jude especially loved the Macy's Flower Show. She could actually smell the fragrances from her rooftop balcony. She felt good, her book tour was amazing, she hit number one and she was leaving for Point Judith in the morning. Yesterday, she sent Aunt Emily a huge gourmet basket filled with gourmet coffees and teas, homemade granola, nuts, seeds and chocolates from around the world. She also thanked Aunt Emily for the lovely bottle of perfume she left when she and Geraldine used her apartment last week. Jude couldn't wait to see David. Last night she dreamt they were on vacation in Spain. They were happy, in love and even more spontaneous then when he was showing her around Point Judith. She had just set her bowl down filled it with yogurt, blueberries and walnuts with a slight drizzle of honey when she heard her cellphone ringing in the living area. She ran to get it only to hear her editor tell her he wanted to see her first thing tomorrow morning. "But, I was going to leave tomorrow," she cried.

"We need to go over these chapters," he proclaimed.

"I'm tired. I just got back from an exhausting book tour. I need to go back to the beach house."

"You're here. Let's get this done and then you can return to the beach."

"I'll be there by nine," she said and tossed the phone on the overstuffed chair. It was bad enough she stayed in the city an extra week to hit a few more book stores and to do the Kelly Clarkson Show. She only had three more weeks left to enjoy the beach house. Jude stood in front of the mirror. "Who the hell are you kidding? You hated the beach house, the beach and the damn kids screaming about sharks, crawfish and snails." Tears streamed down her face. She plopped onto the sofa. "I want to write!" she hollered. "But I love David," she whispered.

Jude ate her breakfast, walked on the treadmill for a half hour and then called David. When she got his voicemail she hung up. She wanted him to give her a reason to return, to choose Point Judith and to be with him. Mostly, she wanted to hear his voice. She spent the rest of the day finishing her chapters for the first book and the chapter layout for the second story. Her new editor insisted on having the entire manuscript a year prior to launch. And now that he is working hand-in-hand with Aunt Emily's publicist the pressure was really on. They both wanted the beta readers, influencers, street teams and book clubs to have the book in their hands six months before the book was even released. Thanks to social media a book's launch has taken on a whole new meaning. It used to be you wrote a book handed it in to your editor then finally to the publisher right before publication, now a book has to go through a whole slew of hands before the cover is actually put on it. "Advance copy," she said aloud before jumping into the shower.

Jude curled up with her laptop and finally wrote the last chapter in book one of the beach series. "There, I hope this makes you happy," she said and closed her laptop. At eight-thirty, her cellphone rang. "David," she said sounding tired but relieved to hear his voice.

"Hello, how's my favorite writer holding up? I'm sorry I missed your call earlier. I left my cellphone in my jacket and had to go back to the construction site to get it. Is everything okay?"

"I miss you," she said in a sleepy voice.

David's heart smiled. "I miss you too. When are you coming back?"

She wanted him to say home. "I was planning on

returning tomorrow, but I have to meet with my editor to go over a few revisions." She took a shot. "By any chance would you like to come here? The city is gorgeous this time of the year. We can go see a show."

Silence. She heard him blow out a long breath before saying, "I can't I have several meetings with the new investors Aunt Emily lined up. I'm sorry, Jude."

"It's fine. I thought I would ask. So I guess I'll see you when I can." She stopped herself from tearing up. Swallowed the lump forming in her throat and said, "Good night, David."

"Good night," he replied knowing he disappointed her.

8

J ude tossed and turned all night. Several times she cried knowing it would never workout. David had his priorities and she has hers. He loved Point Judith too much to ever consider moving to New York. She had to be in the city, her editor, publisher, even Jude's literary agent lived within walking distance. She was close to everyone and everything. She got up, drank a cup of coffee and walked to her editor's office. One look at her and he knew she was totally drained. "You are a hot mess," he said adding, "Did you even comb your hair this morning?"

She offered a smug look, sat down and shook her head. When she began to cry. He got up, closed his door and sat down next to her. "Wow, I'm so sorry." He put an arm around her shoulders and told her it was okay.

"You're not my first rodeo. A lot of authors crash after a long and exhausting book tour."

Jude apologized. "I'm sorry. I should have cleared my head before coming here." Then she bent down and took out her laptop. When she stared out the window, he closed her laptop and moved his chair closer to hers.

"Tell me what's bothering you," he said taking the laptop from her and put it on his desk.

"I'm not cut out for this romance stuff," she cried. Jude looked into his eyes. "I've fallen in love."

"Okay, so you're in love. Great, you can add romance to your repertoire. Women are going to love it. The beach, a romantic escapade and—"

Jude lost it. She couldn't hold back her tears.

"Oh, dear. There's more to it, isn't there?"

"I'm in love with David Wayne and he—" She buried her face in the palms of her hands.

"Your tour guide?"

Jude chuckled aloud. "Yeah, but he's more than that." She shrugged her shoulders and inhaled a deep breath before saying, "David took me to so many wonderful places and not just in Rhode Island." She proceeded to tell him about their trip to Alaska, about all her firsts and how he made her feel every time she saw him. "The more time I spent with him the more I fell in love with him. I miss him so much. I can't bear the thought of not seeing ever again."

"Sweetheart, you fell hard." He raised one shoulder

and said, "I'm jelly about your peanut butter." They both laughed. "Oh, damn, you were supposed to go back today. We can do this over Zoom."

Jude shook her head. "He'll never leave Point Judith. Salt runs in his veins." She shook her head. "He's stuck in the sand and I remain a Manhattanite."

"No you're not! What are you waiting for? Pack your stuff and get the hell out of the city." He shook his head saying, "I can't believe I just said that. Jude, seriously, what are you waiting for? We can do all of our meetings via Zoom. Go back to that cute little beach house and tell him how you feel."

"My lease is up at the end of the month and the realtor already rented it to someone else."

"So buy a damn house in Rhode Island."

She sat stoic. "But, I love the city," she said softly. "What about my apartment?"

"Don't fall in love with real estate. Sell the damn thing. Follow your heart. Now that you've hit number one I'm sure the publisher would pay for your entire stay when you come into Manhattan."

"It's not that. Money isn't the problem." She rubbed her face and moaned.

"Oh, dear. He doesn't know how you feel does he?"

Jude shook her head. "He has a great life. There isn't a day that goes by where he's not busy helping someone. He's always thinking of ways to feed the homeless. He's building an entire community for them." She stood up, moved over to the window and looked down at the street below. "He's the most genuine, loving and caring person I have ever met." She turned to face her editor. "My heart melts every time I see him. The first day I met him he took my breath away and it wasn't just his looks. His friend was in trouble." Jude blew out a long breath before adding, "He bent down, scooped her up and carried her away like they do in the movies." She shook her head. "He's amazing. Long legs, broad shoulders and he is knock down gorgeous." She sat down offered a wry grin. "I immediately Googled him. I wanted to know everything about him and when I read about all of his accomplishments, I was impressed. But after spending one day with him, I saw his heart. He's the real thing. He's every woman's dream, desire and prayer."

Jude's editor got up, picked up her laptop and told her to go to him. "This can wait," he said as he handed her the laptop. "Judith Ann, don't walk, run into his arms, tell him how you feel and make him feel your love."

Jude stood there for a moment, wondering if David felt the same about her as she does him. Several times she caught him looking at her with passion in his eyes. She saw a flicker of hope when they were in Alaska. And when he said his aunt would never believe they didn't care for one another that was another sign. "What if I'm just a women in need of saving?"

"Saving?" He waved his hand at her. "Girl, look at

you. You're gorgeous and if I wasn't a happy gay man I would be totally attracted to you. You're beautiful, you have brains and you have your own damn money. Jude you're successful. You can have any man you want and he would be a fool not to be in love with you." He put his hands on her shoulders. "Listen to me, you are far from a damsel in distress. Why do you think he spent so much time with you? Hello! He wanted to be with you. Trust me, he likes you. Now go and be with your man. And for heaven's sake don't be shy." Then he clapped his hands. "I can see it now. Judith Ann number one romance writer."

Jude laughed. "We're writing a beach series. Remember?" Then she sat down, opened her laptop and said, "I don't want any distractions or anyone bothering me about damn chapters when I get back to Point Judith. I'll have three weeks to convince that man to be mine. So grab your red pen and let's finish this."

Four hours later, Jude and her editor completed all of the revisions on the first book in her new series. Jude hugged him tight. "Thank you for everything, especially for being my friend."

He tapped her on the nose and told her he didn't want to see her until September. "Now go." He pointed to the door. "You're not my only client you know." He winked at her. "But you are my favorite."

On the way back to her apartment she stopped at Katz's Delicatessen for a Reuben sandwich, dill pickle and a bag of chips. "Huh, my first editor demanded I live in the Manhattan, he even sold me my penthouse, now my new editor tells me to leave the city." She grabbed her empty plate, stood up and walked toward the garbage can smiling at the two men staring at her. She stopped at their table. "It's okay, I'm a writer. I get paid to think aloud."

9

The rain finally subsided, but then again rain never stopped David from heading down the beach for his morning run. When he went by Jude's summer rental, he felt a ping in his heart. The lights were still out and she had not returned to Point Judith. He expected her back two days ago. Although he totally understood the importance of her building her book business to a higher level, he was tormented by a deep sense of emptiness, accompanied by a desire to be with her. He returned home, showered, had breakfast and sat out on the back deck. The air was fresh with a hope of the future to come. He inhaled, closed his eyes and promised himself to find a way to get her to stay. He jumped up in time to see her car go by then he undressed and wrapped a towel around his waist. "Crap, my hair." He wet his head and slicked his hair back ever so slightly.

Jude's driver parked the car in front of her rental at ten o'clock sharp. She unpacked, made herself a cup of tea, signed a few more thank you notes and changed her clothes. She was excited to go and see David. She put on a new spring dress and her favorite—Keds sneakers. When her driver drove by David's house earlier, she was glad his Tahoe was in the driveway. She headed down the beach, knocked on the back door, went around to the front and rang the doorbell. With his Tahoe still in the driveway, she wondered if he was out jogging. She was just about to step down off the porch when she heard him say, "Welcome home stranger."

She turned around and saw him standing behind the door. The smile on his face said he was just as happy to see her, as she was him.

"I just got out of the shower. Give me two minutes to get dressed and I'll make us lunch. I want to hear all about your book tour."

Jude stepped up to the front door and followed him toward the living room. "Have a seat, I'll be with you in a minute." Wearing only a towel wrapped around his waist, David headed back into his bedroom to put his shorts and t-shirt back on.

Jude stood in the living room, breathing heavier and heavier. Her chest rising and falling. Her insides were hammering. David's oozing sex appeal was getting to her and his shy mannerism made him even more appealing. Seeing him wrapped up in that towel was a turn on. Jude fanned her dress trying to relieve the mounting hotness she felt. She was so hot; she untied the sweater tied around her neck, stepped out onto the back deck and smiled at the thought of the two of them making love. She breathed into the sweater and allowed an even bigger smile to grace her face.

David stood in front of the mirror grinning, hoping his trick worked. When he saw her car drive by, he gave her just enough time to unpack and show up at his door. He entered the living room and inhaled her beauty. He allowed her to stand there long enough before asking her if she was hungry. "Would you like to join me for lunch? I just prepared a nice garden salad with baby greens, fresh spearmint leaves, mandarin oranges and pomegranate along with pickled onions?"

Jude turned around and when she did, he noticed she was a little red in the face. He smiled. "We'll eat in here. I'll turn the air conditioner on. Come on inside. I have Aunt Emily's homemade vinaigrette dressing that you love so much."

Jude sachet her way towards him, kissed him on the lips, looked into his eyes and said, "I missed you." She giggled. "And yes, I am starving and I do love—"

David returned her kissed on the lips. "I hated not seeing your lights on." He offered a seductive smile adding, "I've missed you more than you can imagine. I'm excited to hear about your time in the city."

"I want to hear what's happening with the new community. Do we have any residents yet?"

David reached over and took Jude by the hand. He kissed the back of it and replied, "We do. Take a seat at the counter and I will tell you everything."

Jude held his hand until he pulled the stool back for her. "I'd like to go and see the progress," she said as she sat down, but then got up, grabbed two glasses and filled them with lemonade. When David tossed in two spearmint leaves, she kissed him on the cheek. "I like it when you spoil me."

He winked at her, set their lunch plates down and returned her kiss. "Eat you lunch and I'll take you to Rhode Island Red's."

She leaned over and hugged him. "I love it and so would he." She fought back tears. Leaned over and rested her head on David's arm. Then she took her first bite and moaned. "Ooo, this is good." She stabbed a pecan and chunk of goat cheese along with a pickled onion. "Who needs to go out to eat when you have your very own private chef? David, this is very tasty."

"I'm glad you like it." He handed her a slice of warm garlic toast. "If we both eat it, we won't be shocked at the bad breath."

They both laughed. "Who cares?" she said and finished

her entire meal. "I've been meaning to ask you, how's your friend, Grace?" She took a sip of her drink adding, "I know she was close to Red and she's pregnant, right?"

"She's wonderful. I'm so happy for her and Steve. Their children get along great and they seem happy."

"Yes, but four kids. Who has the time for all those soccer games, play dates and cookie campaigns?" She laughed.

"Not me," David said and picked up their plates. "Would you like some ice cream? I made a pint of mint chocolate chip first thing this morning."

"That's my favorite. Yes. Please," she replied sounding demure.

"I also made a new batch of amaretto cherry to try. I may have put a little too much amaretto in."

"We'll have that tonight while we watch an episode of Yellowstone."

David's heart smiled just thinking about spending the entire day with her. "I'll take out two filet mignons. Would you like brown rice or a baked potato?"

Jude sat quietly looking into his eyes.

David smiled at her. "What?"

"Nothing," she said and got down off the kitchen stool. "I'm just happy to see you."

David picked up their glasses and wondered if something happened in the city or, was she genuinely happy to be back. "I'm happy to see you too." After they ate their ice cream, he asked her if she was ready. "Shall we go?"

Jude clapped her hands together. "Yes."

David drove listening to Jude tell him how grateful she was to Aunt Emily. "I always thought my writing was enough and my readers were my world, but I have to tell you hitting number one made all my dreams even sweeter." She put her hand on his knee. "I want to help you with the living facility."

David reached down and took hold of her hand, moved it slowly up his thigh and then kissed the back of it. Jude smiled from the inside and laced her fingers in his. "You really did miss me," she teased.

"You know what they say."

"What?" she asked looking at him with anticipation.

He glanced over at her. "If you love something, let it go and if it comes back—"

She took back her hand and swatted him on his leg. "Now, I'm a thing?" Then she took hold of his hand and kiss its palm. "I like being your thing. Just don't call me Miss Thing." They both laughed. "Oh, David. Wow," she said as he turned the corner. "You really are a Godsend."

David parked the Tahoe next to Faith's car, opened the door for Jude and told her he wanted to stop in the office for a moment. "Let me check in with Faith and see what she needs me to do next week."

David held the door open for Jude. Faith jumped to her feet when they walked in. "Hi, wow, you really did come." She held her hand out to Jude. "Thank you so much for your check. It will be put to good use."

David pursed his lips, tilted his head ever so slightly and wondered what just happened. He pointed to Jude. "You spoke to Faith?"

"Yes," she replied. "I want to be a part of all this. Faith said I could take part in the pre-paid program."

David looked at Faith, turning the palms of his hands up.

"I created a monthly donation plan to help fund the pre-paid cards for the residents. People can donate as little as thirty dollars a month or whatever can they afford. The money goes into a separate account that funds the cards."

"I thought it was a fabulous idea," Jude said.

David pointed to Faith. "Genius."

"Thank you. I was telling Jude that Amelia has over twenty people committed to the program."

David looked at Jude. Was she jealous of Amelia? Is that why she was so eager to be a part of the program? To come to the— he stopped himself from thinking it was anything accept good intensions. Then he remembered her putting her arm through his when he was talking to Amelia at the reception. He looked over at Jude and Faith, "Thank you. Both of you."

Jude looked at him wondering if he was okay.

"Oh, David, I'm going to need you to be here next

Wednesday to sign for a delivery," Faith said adding, "Can you be here at nine?"

"Of course," he said, noticing Faith winked at Jude.

"I'd like to come as well." Jude looked at David. "If that's okay with you."

David put his hand on her shoulder. "I would like that." Then he told Faith he was going to show Jude around. "Shall we take a tour?"

Jude raised her eyebrows several times. "Please." She was amazed at not only the progress but the number of vendors. "This is going to make their lives so much richer." She stopped walking for a second and shook her head in aww. On the right an entire street was lined with tiny houses. "David they are adorable." She paused. "What's the difference between the two?"

"Come on, I'll show you." David took her by the hand and walked up to the first home. They stepped up onto the front porch then he held the door open for her to go inside. The home offered a nice size living room, kitchen, bedroom, bathroom and a small laundry room.

Jude stood in the bedroom. "You furnished the entire home—" Tears filled her eyes. David stood behind her, held her tight, and kissed the back of her head as she exhaled a cry. "I am amazed at your willingness to help others." She turned around and buried her face in his chest. "This is so beautiful."

He wiped away her tears, kissed her passionately and said, "God has blessed me with so much. Now it's my turn to share his blessings with those who need it the most." He kissed her again and said, "Thank you for your donation."

She held his face in her hands. Kissed him once, twice, three times before saying, "You're infectious, inspiring and I like being around you."

Over her shoulder David saw an empty bed. As tempted as he was to pick her up right then and there and make love to her, he stopped himself. It wasn't the place nor the time. "If you're not doing anything this weekend, would you like to go up to the cabin with me for the weekend? You can write by the fire, out on the front porch and I promise you there will not be any children to bother you."

Jude shivered from the chill that ran down her spine. Then she smiled a seductive grin and said, "That sounds wonderful. Yes." She raised an eyebrow and winked. "I'll pack my best flannel pajamas." She laughed aloud and wiped away her tears. "What can I bring?"

He kissed her on the nose. "You, your work and yes there will be a pajama party." David showed Jude the two bedroom unit and once again she was amazed at his creativity. He kissed her and whispered in her ear, "Thank you for coming back to me."

10

A soft, golden sunlight streamed through a clear blue sky, casting a warm glow on the still-cool sand, where the gentle lapping of waves against the shore created a soothing rhythm. Jude stood near the water's edge, breathing in the fresh air with a hint of salt and the scent of nearby blooming wildflowers. Overhead seagulls danced, to her right three women were setting up beach umbrellas, providing shade from the not yet too hot, warmth of spring. Thankfully, there were no children in sight. Jude inhaled once more to take in the newly awakened coastline. There was something special about being near the ocean. She couldn't put her finger on it, but she knew... it was special. A breeze made her shiver. She wrapped her arms around herself, looked up and closed her eyes. *I'm in love.*

"Good morning," the voice said from behind her.

Jude turned around and waved to her neighbor, Dr. Ferris. "Good morning."

Dr. Ferris walked up to her. "It's magical, right?"

Jude smiled at him knowing he felt it too. "There's more to those waves than beautiful sunrises and sunsets." When he looked down, she tapped his elbow. "Is everything okay?" He smiled at her, nodding intently. "Dr. Ferris?"

"Please, call me Dan." Then he pointed out toward a passing sailboat. "I thought I was ready, clearly, I am not. I figured when I retired, I would go fishing, spend more time learning something new. The other day, I went clamming. I couldn't eat them all. I went for a long walk down the beach and saw a gorgeous sunset, but there was no one to share it with. I've decided to sell the beach house and go back to work."

"I'll miss you, but I totally understand. I don't think I will ever stop writing; I love it so much."

He offered her a gentle smile. "Before I put the house back on the market, I thought I would ask you if you were interested in buying it."

"Oh, wow. Umm, thank you?" She raised her eyebrows. "I appreciate your offer; however, I too will be returning to the city soon."

Dr. Ferris turned and looked toward David's house. "Are you sure?" He pointed down the beach. "Life is too precious to let an opportunity like David Wayne slip away. How about I give you a few days to think about my offer."

Jude inhaled as she watched him slowly turn to leave, then she stared at David's home wondering how her heart would feel when her lease was up. "Wow, I only have a few weeks left." She sat down on the beach, brought her knees up to her chest, hugged them and buried her face thinking about the past year, renting a house on the beach so she could write a new series of novels. She never expected to fall in love. Jude sat up and looked at David's house one more time before going inside. She started to make herself a cup of tea when she thought, *you're a writer, write him a love letter.* Jude sipped her tea, writing to David. "There, I've professed my love to you."

Ava couldn't wait to call David. She was holding her first design in her hands and it felt good to be back at doing what she loved. Shelby walk up from behind her and said, "He's going to love it."

Ava jumped. "Geez, you scared the crap out of me."

Shelby laughed at her. "You seriously need to get used to living with someone." Then she grabbed a travel mug of coffee and told Ava she was heading out to discover new backdrops. "I'll see you later, I'm going to visit a few parks and beaches." She kissed Ava goodbye, waved and headed for the door.

Ava shouted to her. "Hey, check out Long Beach. I love you."

Shelby stopped, turned around and walked back over to Ava. "How much?"

Ava put the coat down and took off her tee shirt, dropped her panties on the floor and said, "This much." Then she ran into the bedroom."

Shelby followed her, stood in the doorway and she too got undressed. An hour later, as they lie in bed talking about how happy they both were, Ava asked Shelby to marry her. Shelby rolled over onto her side, face to face the women slowly nodded their heads. Shelby knew Ava was serious and for the first time in her life she was just as happy. Ava wiped away a tear from Shelby's face. Then she shed her own tears. "I love you, Shelby. Marry me."

Shelby rolled back over, opened her nightstand drawer and handed Ava two tickets to Cabo San Lucas, Mexico. Ava read them, held the tickets to her chest and openly cried. Shelby hugged her and said, "Yes, I will marry you in Cabo. I can't believe you asked *me*. I was planning on asking you."

After they showered, got dressed, Ava said she wanted it to be just the two of them. "We'll elope. We don't need anyone. We'll send everyone a photo." She laughed. "Besides Grace and Ella have a lot going on right now."

"Are you sure?" Shelby said as she tossed Ava an avocado. "They offer a great wedding package for up to fifty guests."

"I'm positive," Ava said as she smashed the fruit and spread it on her toast.

Shelby kissed her goodbye and told her to call David. "Don't forget to call David and be sure to tell him I said hi."

Ava took a bite of her breakfast and held up her phone. When she finished eating, she called David.

"Hello, Ava," David said.

"I have good news. The coats are done and we had a size six and a larger woman try them on. They love the draw string. I tried it on and it feels like being wrapped up in a cozy blanket."

"Wow that was fast. How many can you produce?"

"How many do you want?" she replied and set her plate in the sink.

"Let's start with three-hundred and see how far they go." He thought for a minute and then asked her, "What about the men's jackets?"

"I should have a sample by the end of the week. I'll get right on manufacturing the women's coats now. David—"

David looked up and saw it was nearly eleven o'clock. He grabbed the set of plans and the contract for the new vendor and said, "Yes?"

"Thank you for believing in me. It means the world to me."

"Ava, everything you touch turns to gold. Your

designs are making fashion history. Promise me one thing, always believe in yourself and—"

She interrupted him by saying, "No more drugs?"

"That's not at all what I was going to say. Take care of Shelby, she's the salt of the earth."

"Can you keep a secret?" she said and held her hand to her mouth surprised she was telling David and not Grace or Ella.

"For you anything," he replied.

"I asked Shelby to marry me and she said yes. We're eloping and getting married in Cabo."

"I am so happy for the two of you. Congratulations and yes, your secret is safe with me. I can't wait to see the photos. You're both going to make the most beautiful brides."

"Thank you, I'll call you next week when I know more about the men's coats."

"Bye for now," he said.

"David. Wait. Shelby wanted me to tell you she said hi."

David offered a warm smile. "Please tell your bride I said hello." He disconnected the call and shook his head. *Everyone is getting married. I seriously need to make my move, either she stays, or she's going back to the big city.* As soon as he got in his car, his cellphone rang. "Jude." He picked up his cell and answered her call. "I was just thinking about you."

"I like that," she said and then asked him, "Are we still going up to your cabin this weekend?"

"I hope so," he replied and smiled from the inside out. "When would you like to leave?"

"How about tomorrow morning, I can be ready by nine."

"Sounds great. Bring your laptop, you can do all the writing you want."

"Are you even real?" she teased. "Do you know how many men are so jealous of their spouse's?"

"I would never stop you from doing what you love. Jude, bring your laptop. I'll pick you up tomorrow," he said and went to hang up.

"David, I'm excited to be spending time with you. I'll meet you at the front door wearing the biggest smile you have ever seen."

"And that's all, right?" He laughed. "I'm kidding. You'll give the neighbors a heart attack. Enjoy the rest of your day, sweetheart." David hung up the phone feeling good about the weekend. "I think we can make this happen." He glanced at his reflection in the mirror. "She's worth every trick in the book."

11

Friday morning, David woke to the sound of spring birds chirping outside his window. He turned the coffee pot on, went jogging and returned home to pack a few things to bring up to the cabin. He needed to go over the vendor contracts and the list of donors Aunt Emily emailed him about. Next, he sent the grocery store a list of items to be delivered to the cabin. He called Henry and told him about the food delivery and asked him to turn the hot tub on and to turn the pool temperature to eighty-five. At eight, he packed the Tahoe and waved to his neighbor as she power walked past him. The air was crisp, offering a refreshing start to a beautiful, invigorating and hopefully a romantic weekend. At a quarter to nine, David pulled up to Jude's. He stepped out in time to see her set two luggage bags outside the door. She waved and held up one finger. When she went back inside, he grabbed her bags and put them in the back along with his.

"Good morning," she called out to him. "It's gorgeous." She walked up to him, handed him her black leather case. "I can't forget this." Then she kissed him on the cheek.

David offered a tantalizing grin. "Good morning to you," he said and closed the hatch. "Are you ready?" He pointed his finger at her. "You didn't forget anything did you?"

"Nope, I have everything," she replied and then asked if they could stop and grab some beer. "Can we stop at the store so I can buy Corona Sun brew, and some oranges?"

David raised an eyebrow. "I already took care of it." Then he opened the car door for her to get in. "Let the relaxation begin," he said and closed the door.

"David, you know what I love about the cabin?" She buckled her seatbelt and proceeded to tell him all the things that she adored about his cabin. "You created such a cozy environment. Seriously, from the thick wood, stone fireplace, leather furniture that I just want to sink my teeth into."

David pulled out onto Ocean Drive and laughed. "You mean your ass, right?" Then he rested his hand on her knee.

She slapped his leg. "I especially love the exposed

beams," she said and then appeared to be lost in thought as a warm expression spread through her.

David glanced over at her. She was everything he ever wanted. She's comfortable and confident in her own skin, she accepts her strengths and her flaws and best of all she boast an inner peace. "You know what I like about you? I like the fact that you embrace your life choices, you pursue your passion with fire and an enthusiasm like I have never seen." He reached over and took her hand in his. Kissed her fingertips and said, "And you always smell good."

She laughed aloud. "You ass, that's my dish soap. Mrs. Meyers-Peony fragrance." Then she leaned over and gave him another kiss on the cheek. "I'm excited about spending some time alone. I promise not to work the entire weekend." Smiling to herself.

"Jude, I told you. That's one of the things I like about you. You're following your heart's desire. Hey, wait a minute. I'm not just a test subject for one of your romance novels, am I?"

"Ha-ha, that depends," she said in her most seductive voice.

"Yeah, well, I plan on being a total gentleman the entire weekend."

"Not if I can help it," she said. "Did I mention I like the hardwood floors and the braided rugs?"

"So, you're going up to the cabin to get decorating ideas?"

She rested her head on his shoulder. David drove in silence... beautiful, comfortable, shared silence. When they reached the gate, she sat up and watched David punch in the code. She rubbed her hands together. "We are going to have so much fun this weekend."

"I hope so, because I ordered a lot of beer."

She whispered in his ear. "I forgot to tell you, I had a tubal ligation, so I hope you didn't buy any condoms."

David stopped the car in the middle of the driveway, turned to face her and kissed her on the lips. When they couldn't breathe, they both smiled. "I didn't offer to help you just so you would sleep with me," he said.

"David, I am not offering to pay you with sex." She laughed. "Although, I did want you to take me to the spring festival this year. Besides, I'm a big girl... some might say a woman. I know what I am doing and I sure as hell know what I want and right now, I want you."

They kissed once more before driving up to the cabin. David parked the Tahoe and took her hand in his. "I'm not looking for a summer fling. I—"

"I know what you're looking for and trust me I want the same thing. Right now, I want a cold beer and then I would like to go for a nice walk with you in the woods. Then I would like to sit by the large window and admirer all the views nature has to offer." She looked into his eyes. "You're going to hold my hand, right?"

"Not if a bear is on our trail, then I'm pushing you in front of me," he teased and opened his car door.

She got out and yelled at him. "David Wayne. I'm telling Aunt Emily what you said. That's not funny." She closed her door and cautiously looked around. "Are there a lot of bears up here?"

David grabbed their luggage, opened the door for her and asked if she wanted lunch before they go hiking. "I ordered a spinach salad for lunch. Would you like to eat before we go for our walk?" Then he opened the fridge and took out two beers. He tapped his to hers. "Cheers."

Jude kissed him on the lips and whispered, "Cheers." in his ear. Then she took a sip and said, "Ahh. Umm, I can wait to eat if you can."

"Okay, let's sit by the fire pit, drink our beer, change our footwear and take a hike."

David and Jude sat by the crackling sound of the fire, with the soft murmur of conversation about their dreams and desires for one another. Jude inhaled listening to David talk about wanting to share his life with her. "The first time I saw you, I wanted to get to know you." He looked at her with an intensity full of desire. "But, as soon as I heard you were only in Point Judith for a year, I—"

Jude set her beer down, got up and sat on David's lap. "Shhhh, this is only the beginning. Let's see where this weekend goes."

"Weekend?" David shook his head. "I'm looking for forever."

"So am I," she whispered and kissed him. "I know what want." She winked. "I can honestly say, I'm ready for a long-term relationship." Then she reached over and held up her empty bottle. "One more and then we'll go hiking with the bears. I need to build my courage up." She stood up and went to the kitchen. Grabbed two slices of orange, squeezed them in their bottles and handed him his bottle. "I remember when you said hello to me but then walked away. I wanted more of you. A lot more."

"Hey, Ava was in trouble," he said and tapped his beer to hers. "Here's to no one bothering us, to long walks, dancing in the rain and kissing under the light of the moon."

"I like the way you think. Okay, now I'm hungry."

When they both finished their lunch, they changed into their hiking shoes and headed out the door. Hand in hand, they hiked along the trail. Thankfully, the only critter they encountered was a deer. "Do I have time to take a bath before dinner?"

"I'll tell you what, you take a nice long bath while I cook," he replied and kissed her tenderly.

While David cooked baked cod fish fillets, rice and custard for dessert; Jude took a nice long bubble bath. At seven in the evening, she stood in the doorway, watching David as he set the table, singing "Ain't Nothing Like The Real Thing" when he twirled around and noticed her, he nodded. Jude was posing in a new pair of flannel pajamas boasting red hot peppers. David smiled at her. Used his index finger to call her over to him. "You take my breath away. I love them," he said and they kissed.

"Can I do anything?"

"Would you grab us each a beer," he replied. "Dinner is almost done."

"Your wish is my command." She walked over to the refrigerator and pointed toward the counter. "Is that egg custard?"

"It is," he replied and set the cod fish and rice on their plates. "I also made a nice gourmet salad."

After dinner they snuggled close together on the sofa, sipping brandy. David asked if she wanted to play a game of cards or checkers. When he beat her three times at checkers, Jude said, "Poker. Strip poker." Then she smiled, knowing how sexy her bra and matching white lace panties were.

"Game on," David said and opened the drawer to get the deck of cards out. "Shall I deal or would you like to—"

Jude gabbed the cards from his grip, fanned them three times and said, "Cut them."

"Oh, man. I'm in trouble," he said, cut the deck and handed them back to her.

Jude doled out their cards, laughed and asked, "What do you have on under that shirt?"

"Nothing," he replied sounding scared.

When Jude won the first game, she made David take off his shirt. "Slowly, please."

David laughed. Stood up and removed his shirt. When Jude won the second hand, she instructed David to take his pants off. "Quickly," she said. "I want to—"

"You're a frigging card shark," David said as he tossed his pants over the chair next to him.

Jude smiled at his boxer briefs. Pointed her finger at him and told him she liked his underwear.

"Are you sure?" he replied. "Because I can take them off too if you'd like."

"Not yet cowboy. I'll let you know when." When Jude won the third hand, she told David to follow her to the hot tub. Once there, she slowly removed her pajamas. Then she climbed into the hot tub wearing her bra and matching white lace panties and said, "Now, please."

"No, way," he said. "You kept yours on."

"Yeah, because I won. When you win, you can make the rules." She leaned back and closed her eyes as he entered the hot tub.

12

David and Jude sat out on the front porch wearing matching white terrycloth robes, stargazing, pointing out constellations and sharing their dreams for the future. "So, what's next for my favorite bestselling author?"

She offered a seductive smile. "Besides loving you?"

The wind was blowing in his favor and every time he inhaled he could smell her shampoo. "What is that scent?" he asked as he moved a lock of hair behind her ear. "It's refreshing."

Jude offered a wide grin. "California Baby." Then she raised an eyebrow. "Calendula flowers. Ever since I moved to Rhode Island I have been using all their products. Shampoo, conditioner and moisturizer. It's great for swimmers."

"Well, it smells amazing on you." David stood up reached out for her hand and told her, "Dance with me." He held her tight in his arms and when he whispered in her ear, "I love you," he heard a sensual whimper come out of her.

Jude nuzzled her face in his neck, feeling the warmth of his skin and the scent of his aftershave. She swallowed the lump in her throat, wiped away a tear and told him, "I honestly thought I would be single for the rest of my life. I never thought I would find a man like you. I'm falling in love with David Wayne."

David and Jude danced three dances before going inside. After David stoked the fire, Jude sat down on the sofa and patted the seat next to her, then she tossed the throw blanket over their legs. "I could live in this cabin forever and it wouldn't bother me if I never saw another soul."

David sat up, looked at her and said, "I can't sell the beach house. My father built it for my mother—"

"David, I love the beach house. I'm just saying I like the quietness the cabin offers."

He sat back and exhaled. "Oh, good." Then he filled their glasses with more brandy. "Question for you. How's your pool game?"

She smiled and said, "Care to make any wagers?"

"Yes, looser has to donate their losses to the community center for a new pool table."

"Game on. How much is a new table?" she asked and sipped her brandy. "Smooth."

"About thirty-grand," he replied.

Jude raised her eyebrows several times. "Tomorrow night, I plan on watching you write that check. But if I—"

He kissed her, caressed her neck, breast and when his hand moved to the notch between her legs, she put her empty glass down on the end table. She gasped, covering her mouth in surprise feeling excited, sensual and ready to spend the rest of her life with him by her side.

At ten o'clock, David stood up, held his hand out to her and asked if she was ready for round two. Jude stood in front of him. She raised her eyebrows and asked how many rounds he could go. Her eyes went wide, then she laughed. "No seriously, I'm good after the second."

"I'll stop whenever you tell me too." He kissed her temple, then he picked her up and carried her into the bedroom.

When he set her down on the bed, she told him she had a confession to make. "I'm not very good at this." She quivered. "Compared to my female friends, I suck at love making." She raised an eyebrow. "I haven't been with a lot of men, so I don't really know what to do, besides missionary style."

David pulled back the covers and said, "We'll learn

together." He tilted his head to the right and held up his right hand. "I can count the number of women I have slept with on one hand."

That night, David held Jude in his arms. Together they laughed about secretly wanting the other person. "I thought I was going to have an orgasm in your living room when I saw you wearing only that damn towel."

"If we're bearing our souls, I should tell you." He paused to capture her beauty as the moonlight cast light upon her face. "You are so beautiful." Then he squeezed her tighter. "From the first day I saw you, I wanted to hold you in my arms and make all your dreams come true."

Jude closed her eyes and whispered, "You already have. Good night, my love." Five minutes later, she was snoring.

David laughed to himself as he thought about sharing his life with her, and yes, listening to her snore every night for the rest of his life was a gift he planned on keeping.

The next morning, David woke up to an empty bed. He lie on his back, knowing she was out there somewhere in the cabin, doing what she loved—writing her heart out. He got up, dressed and headed out the door. An hour later, he returned, sat in the kitchen and drank a cup of coffee. At ten o'clock he found Jude in the pool house, sitting in a lounge chair with her laptop on her lap, typing away. He slowly backed out showered and went back to the kitchen. At noon, Jude smelled something delicious cooking. She stretched out her arms, set the laptop down and stood up.

David was standing at the sink, rinsing dishes when Jude wrapped her arms around his waist. "Good morning, handsome."

David turned around, kissed her and asked, "How did you sleep?"

He took in a deep breath. "Like a bear in her den. Did my snoring keep you awake all night?" She laughed. "My college roommate had to wear earbuds; my snoring was so loud."

"Well, I found it to be very soothing. Besides, I too snore. You sound like a baby compared to me. Sometimes, I wake myself up. Would you like some breakfast?"

"I think I'll have some avocado toast and then I need to either do yoga or go hiking," she said.

"We can do whatever you would like to do," he replied.

"No," Jude said as she put two pieces of Dave's Killer Bread in the toaster.

His lips parted as if he was going to respond, but then he snapped them closed and thought for a minute. "No?" he said and held his hands up.

"David, if this going to work, we need to do what makes both of us happy. I don't want you catering to me twenty-four-seven. I want to make you happy. I want to get to know you more. Do the things that you like to do?" She grabbed her toast and started spreading the avocado on them. Then she took her first bite, waiting for him to reply with a suggestion. "Well?" then she smiled at him.

Her smile took his breath away. "Hmm, I'm not sure who sent you to me, but I am forever grateful. Jude, I may not have slept with a lot of women in my day, but I have dated enough to know that you are a rare fine." He rubbed her back as he told her he had a few more contracts to go over so if she wanted to do yoga that would be great. "Then, I am all yours."

That afternoon, David took Jude out for a ride in the paddleboat around the entire lake. Every time she leaned back and closed her eyes, his heart smiled. When she answered a text, he smiled and winked at her. She set her phone down and said, "Thank you."

"For what?" he asked.

"For not getting upset with me for working while we are together."

"Jude, I respect you and that means I respect the work that you do. You'll never have to worry about me being jealous of your work or your work husband."

Jude laughed. "Work husband?" She shook her head. "My editor is gay, my literary agent is a woman and just so you know, we were talking about you. I was telling her how much I love you and how you make me feel so special." She got up, almost tipping the paddleboat over and rested her head on his lap, looked up and said, "Being with you is like being on vacation every day. I feel so relaxed and—"

He leaned down and kissed her lips.

"Happy," she said.

"I'm glad. I feel the same way about you. And we get to build this life together."

During dinner, Jude asked David if he ever thought about being with Grace. "You know, like this."

David shook his head. "Never, I respected her and besides, she was like a sister to me. We never looked at each other that way." He blew out a breath. "She was broken when I met her. I think Red had a better chance at getting her to open her heart."

She kissed him on the cheek. "I'm a simple woman. I don't need a lot. I'm not a big jewelry person." She looked into his eyes. "Promise me, you will love me—"

He picked her up and carried her to the living room, looked into her eyes and said, "I will love you till the day I die."

She shook her head. "I don't ever want that day to come. I'm not sure I could bear the burden of living without you."

They kissed, held one another and fell asleep in each other's arms.

The next day, she was emailing her literary agent when she asked David, "My agent wants to send me some books, do you mind if I give her this address?"

"Of course," he said and told her the address.

Jude typed in the address and set her phone down. "What would you like to do today?" she stretched out her arms.

"Would you like to go fishing in the canoe?"

"Sure," she said and got up.

"If you want to bring your laptop or—"

"A book," she replied.

"Exactly." Then he pointed to her nightgown and said, "You might want to change."

Jude had her game face on. "Is it nice outside?"

"Gorgeous. It was seventy-four when I went jogging."

"Okay, I'll put on a pair of shorts and a T-shirt." She grabbed her Keds, book and sunscreen. She was tying up her sneakers when David said he packed a cooler.

"I put a few beers and bottles of water in it along with a couple protein bars and a container of berries."

Jude shook her head, looked up and said, "Thank You." Then she pointed her finger at David. "Not you, Him. For allowing you to live alone long enough to know how to cook, clean up after yourself and for being so caring."

David winked at her and said, "Don't get mad God, but my aunt taught me as well."

Jude smiled. "Yes, she did."

Jude and David paddled around the entire lake. David watched as Jude read her book, allowed the sun to warm her face and tan her legs. She smiled every time she caught him looking at her. "No wonder you haven't caught anything," she teased. "What are you looking at?"

"My future, and the most beautiful woman I have ever met. You have a radiant glow today."

She smiled, pointed her finger at him. "You make me feel beautiful. David, I know I am not a beautiful woman, but I have to say, you make me feel like I am." She went to move closer to him, but the canoe rocked and her book fell into the water.

David dived in, grabbed the book and held it up to her. When she reached for it, he pulled her into the water. "I've got you," he said and told her to wrap her legs around his waist. "Are you cold?"

"She shook her head, looked into his eyes and said, "It's so refreshing. I'm good."

David swam on his back with Jude on his chest the whole time. Then she rolled off and showed him her moves. She swam by herself. He clapped his hands. "Wow, look at you," he said and followed her to the water's edge. Jude collapsed on grass as David lie next to her.

"I've been practicing every day," she said and sat up. "I swim in the morning while you are out jogging." Across the lake they saw Henry mowing. Jude waved to him. "Is that your caretaker?"

"That's Henry. We went to high school together. He's

a great guy. He lives in the gate house and yes, he takes care of the place."

"I saw him stacking firewood on the back porch the other day. He's good looking. Is he single?"

"Hey, where are you going with this?" David laughed.

"Relax," she said. "By the way, I like seeing you jealous. My literary agent is looking for love and they seem to be about the same age."

"Yeah, I think Henry is content being alone. I'm not sure why, but he enjoys being on his own."

"What does he do all day? Does he work?"

"He takes care of the cabin in exchange for free rent. He enjoys hunting, fishing and he too hikes the trails. And he forges for mushrooms, berries and leafy greens."

"Greens? In the woods?" She asked as she watched Henry mow up a hill.

David smiled and said, "Yes, dandelions, chicory and he loves fiddleheads."

Her belly grumbled. "Can we go forging for berries?" she asked and moved closer to him.

"Ahh, you're going to love spending time up here. We have blackberries, blueberries and raspberries over by the sunny field at the top of the hill. I have a baseball cap you can wear." Then he laughed aloud before saying, "I'll grab the bullhorn in case we encounter any bears."

"Bears?" She waved her hand at him. "Now you're

just making fun of me." She leaned back and looked into his eyes. "Right?"

David chuckled. "No, it's spring and that means momma bear and her new cubs will be roaming the woods."

"I'll buy my berries at Whole Foods," she said.

13

Wednesday morning, Faith called David to remind him to be at the facility by nine. "David, don't be late today."

"I'll be there," he replied and then went in search for Jude.

David entered the pool house, but she wasn't there. When he turned around he bumped right into her. "You better get dressed or we'll be late," she said, looking prettier than the day before. She was wearing a pair of navy blue linen shorts and a matching vest that enhanced her waistline perfectly. She traded her Keds in for a pair of Larroudè sandals with sparkling blue gemstones.

"You're gorgeous." He kissed her tenderly and said, "Shorts it is. I have the perfect shirt too." He walked back to the bedroom, got dressed and then found Jude waiting for him on the front porch holding David's camcorder.

She smiled and said, "I love it." David was wearing khaki shorts and a button down shirt with navy blue fishing hooks.

On the drive to the new site they saw daffodils and tulips blooming in front yards and along the highway, wildflowers were in abundance. The sweet scent of flowers was everywhere and when they got out of the Tahoe, the chirping birds were singing to the peepers. The days were longer and that meant John and his crew were busier than ever. "So why the camcorder?" he asked as he turned in time to see everyone standing outside the office. "Jude, what's going on?"

Jude got out of the vehicle and smiled. As soon as she waved to Faith she saw Amelia standing next to John. "You didn't tell me Amelia was coming today?"

David closed her door and replied, "I had no idea she was coming here today. I'm sure she's here to see Faith." Then he took Jude in his arms, gave a hug and whispered in her ear. "I'm in love with you." He kissed her tenderly on the lips. Took her by the hand and walked toward everyone. Before they reached the crowd, David saw the convoy. "Wow," he said and Jude hugged him even tighter. "Faith wanted to surprise you."

David watched as the trucks made their way down every road delivering the last of the homes. Jude looked at him. "You did it and I'm so stinking proud of you."

A moment later, Amelia introduced David and Jude to three more investors. "Okay, we need to get back to the hospital," Amelia said and waved goodbye to Faith.

After they got back in the car, David said he had an idea. Jude loved it and by one o'clock that afternoon, David and Jude drove straight to Henry Bears' Park toy store and then to Hasbro Children's Hospital to hand out stuffed animals and books to the children. When they got back in his Tahoe, Jude had tears in her eyes. "You are such a blessing. Those children looked at you like you were Superman."

David pulled the car over to the side of the road. Leaned over and kissed her. "I am so glad you are by my side. As long as we are together, we can do—"

She kissed him and cried, "I don't know what came over me, but seeing those children."

"I know," he said. "I felt the same way. Hey, I have an idea. Let's take a drive up to Vermont this weekend. We'll do nothing at all and everything in between. We'll get out of town and explore New England." Then he wiped away her tears.

Jude inhaled. "I love the idea. So much that I am leaving my laptop home. I want to discover so much with you, Mr. Wayne."

David smiled. "Please call me David."

She swatted his leg and kissed him. "I need to use a bathroom. Can we stop somewhere?"

David pulled into the Hemenway's Restaurant in

Providence. Jude jumped out of the vehicle and instructed him to order her a beer and whatever appetizer he was willing to share with her. "Remember, I will eat anything," she said and asked the hostess where the restrooms were.

David sat at the table, order their drinks and the assorted hot seafood platter with fried calamari, bacon wrapped scallops and stuffies. Jude sat down in time to toast the occasion. "Here's to new homes and—"

"Too many firsts for both of us." He looked around the room. "I like this place. It's a first for me." then he tapped his bottle to hers. "Cheers."

"Cheers. So what should I pack for this weekend?"

David set his glass down and offered a devilish grin. "Would you care to go shopping?" he asked as he felt her foot move up his leg. "I know exactly what I'm buying you," he said.

"What?" she asked laughing as she put her foot back on the floor just as their server set their starter down in the center of the table.

"Do you need more time to look at the menu," he asked and Jude picked up her menu.

"David, do you know what you're ordering," she asked.

David told her he wanted the Maine lobster with crab stuffing and then nodded to the waiter to give her a second.

Jude looked up from the menu and ordered the

yellowfin tuna and asked if they could share a mixed baby greens salad.

"Of course," the waiter said adding, "Enjoy your appetizer, I'll back in a few."

"That was so nice of Amelia to stop by," he said as Jude's eyebrows rose higher.

"Yes," Jude said her voice barely a whisper. Then she stabbed a bacon wrapped scallop and put it in her mouth.

David's eyes opened wide watching her try to chew the very large bite. Then he picked up his cellphone and looked up women's clothing boutique in Providence. He added the address to his GPS and said, "Perfect. Queen of Hearts."

Jude pulled the fork back out of her mouth. "Excuse me?"

"The store. It's perfect for a weekend in Vermont."

Jude smiled and tilted her head. "I'm buying every sexy outfit they have. I intend on driving you mad this weekend."

David laughed. "Lord, she wants to kill me."

In the store Jude purchased a leopard bra with matching panties and garter along with a black sun dress and a pair of denim overalls. "In case you take me cow tipping."

"Hey no need to take your frustration out on the cows. There will be no tipping cows over."

They walked out of the boutique hand in hand,

laughing about David needing his own pair of overalls. "I wish we had a cooler in the car," he said. "I would have liked to bring the leftovers home for dinner."

"I can cook, you know."

David opened the hatch, put her bags inside and said, "And you owe me a round of pool."

As Jude opened the car door she said, "I'll cook while you grab your checkbook." When David got in the car Jude told him she was cooking her famous home-made pasta with sausage and mushrooms. "We need to stop at the store so I can buy some sweet and hot sausage?"

After dinner, Jude and David played pool. No one won. They both quit as soon as they heard a knock on the door. But when David opened it he didn't see anyone. "That's strange. You heard it too, right?"

"Yes," she replied and said she was tired. "I'm exhausted, I think I'll turn in."

David followed her to the bedroom. It was past midnight when he thought he heard another sound coming from the front porch. He slowly pulled his arm out from under Jude's side and slide out of the bed. He walked around the entire house looking outside, listening for any noise. A half hour later he went back to bed. At three o'clock, David jumped out of bed and ran to the back porch. Out in the distance he could see a black bear and three baby cubs. Jude crept up behind him, wrapped her arms around him and scared him.

David jumped, spun around and laughed. "Momma bear has discovered the sedges." He pointed to the row of ornamental grasses along the outdoor kitchen.

"Oh," Jude replied and stood closer. "I'll bet it was her earlier too. That's the same grass in front of the house."

David held her tight in his arms. "It was probably one of the cubs up on the porch. Let's go back to sleep," he said and she agreed.

When Jude woke up, David was already sitting at the kitchen counter. He turned to kiss her. "Can I get you a cup of coffee?"

"I can get it," she replied and poured herself a cup before refilling his. "What are you working on today?"

David closed the laptop and said, "I just made our reservations for the weekend."

Jude leaned over and kissed his cheek. "I'm leaving my laptop home. I want to enjoy every second with you."

After breakfast David packed the Tahoe and asked Jude if she had everything. "Are you sure you don't want to bring your laptop?"

"Nope, I have plans." She winked and tossed him a plum.

David and Jude drove for three hours straight, singing along with the radio, talking about their most embarrassing moments, their interests and their hopes and dreams. "We should go away every month," David said. "We need to explore New England. I've traveled the world and yet I have never been to Vermont." He turned to face her for a second. "What?"

She was looking at him with love in her heart and appreciation in her soul. "I'm happy."

He took her hand in his and said, "So am I. Jude, the more I am with you the more I want to spend every second discovering new, exciting moments with you."

She offered a crimson smile. "Can I share a little secret with you?"

"Of course," he said and turned on Main Street in Vermont.

"This is the first time in my life that I didn't have to worry. As a child I worried about my family. And when I'm writing I wonder if my readers are going to like my stories, but when I am with you, I'm free all worry."

David pulled up to the Weston, parked in front of the green awning and turned the vehicle off. "I promise to love you for the rest of my life and together we are going to discover more firsts than you can imagine."

Jude wiped away the tear falling from her eye. "I love you, David and I intended on making you feel my love every day. Starting right now." She handed him a small box. "Open it."

David pursed his lips. Inside were two matching eternal bond engraved bracelets. He read the inscriptions. "Forever and Always."

David placed Jude's on her wrist and when she took

his and put it on his wrist he told her. "They're perfect. Just like you."

Inside, the man at the front desk greeted them with a pamphlet and invitation to a wine tasting at six o'clock in the wine room. "Mr. and Mrs. Wayne we hope you enjoy your stay. By the way, you're all set for your two o'clock couples massage in the spa."

David heard Jude say, "Oh yeah."

Their room was gorgeous. Sitting on a small round table in front of the fireplace were two glasses a bottle of Michter's 25 Year Kentucky Straight Bourbon. Jude stood in front of the window looking out. "It's gorgeous here. I just want to sit in those Adirondack chairs and breathe in the country air. Oh, David look at that garden. It's blooming robust colors everywhere."

David was about to ask her what she wanted to do first, but instead he suggested they take a tour of the grounds. "I'd like to go for a walk and check out the place before our massage. What do you say?"

"Great idea. Let's stretch our legs." When Jude saw the wet bar, she pointed to it. "Would you like a water?"

"Sure."

Jude opened the fridge and saw it was stocked with fresh berries, oranges and beer. On the table was a welcome basket filled with gourmet chocolates, French cookies, cheese and crackers. She placed her hand over her heart. "I get you all to myself this weekend."

David chuckled. "Forever and always." Then he took

her by the hand and headed outside. They waved to a couple playing bocce ball and strolled hand in hand through the gardens and when they saw the patio they knew they wanted to have lunch there.

"This place is so beautiful I want to sleep in a tent so I can enjoy all of its beauty," she said.

"I imagined us soaking in the tub, having dinner by the fireplace and—"

"Making love until we can't breathe," she whispered in his ear.

"Huh, I was going to say candlelight, but I like your idea better.

After their massage they both sat in the sauna for an hour. Jude had David laughing so hard he cried. She told him about the time she walked out of Macy's with the back of her dress tucked into her underwear. "I had no idea until a woman yelled at me to stop and pulled the dress down. It was so embarrassing."

"Oh, I would have paid to see that," he said and wiped his eyes.

Jude swatted his lag. "I'll bet you would have. Okay, I'm hot."

David stepped into the men's shower room and Jude headed for the ladies'. When they reached their room, Jude said she still wanted to soak in the tub. "My massage therapist was great, but I think it's been too long since I had one, I'm going to soak my bones for a while."

David sat down in the chair next to the library. Put his index finger over his top lip and nodded. "Sounds good." Then he poured each of them a glass of bourbon. When she stood in the doorway and used her finger to invite him in, he picked up the glasses and joined her. Jude rested her head on David's chest, sipping her cocktail.

Every time she let out an "Mmmm." David kissed the back of her head. "Let's skip the wine tasting tonight and have dinner in our room," she said. "We'll sit by the fire and plan our next trip."

David and Jude lie on the bed in their matching robes feeling more relaxed than either of them had felt in a long time. "I'm glad we have the whole weekend ahead of us," he said and she wondered what else he had up his sleeve. "How about we alternate our trip plans. I picked this one so it's your turn to plan our next vacation."

"Deal," she said and took off her robe. When she straddled his hips, he inhaled and opened his robe just enough for her to feel his excitement. "Teach me how to satisfy you this way?" She shrugged her shoulders, her cheeks still red from soaking in a hot tub. "I only know one position."

David reached under her buttocks and gently moved her up and down. A minute later, Jude had him moaning. When she collapsed onto his chest he whispered in her ear. "Wow." He kissed her. "You're a fast learner."

She rolled off and lie next to him. "It was all you, the guy who told me I was terrible at sex, had to hold onto his penis all the time or he went limp." She sat up and looked over her shoulder. "You on the other hand." She stood up and headed for the bathroom, stopped at the door, held onto the door jam and said, "Your throbbing, swollen manhood—"

When he jumped up, she ran into the shower.

14

They woke to rain pelting their windows. David asked if she wanted to order room service. Jude rolled closer to him, rested her head on his chest and told him she wanted to go downstairs and tour the rooms. "Would you like to check out the rest of the inn?"

"Sounds good," he responded and then lifted the covers exposing their naked bodies. "Maybe we should put some clothes on." He scrunched his nose and laughed when she shook her head.

"I need a shower." She got up and grabbed her toiletry bag before going into the bathroom. When she came back out and said, "They have two shower heads. Come on, I promise not to take advantage of you." She offered a Cat-like Smile. "But, it would be nice if you washed my back."

David shook his head. "Oh, I plan on washing more than your back," he teased.

"Hahaha, just don't get soap in my eyes."

Downstairs they met a lovely couple from Dover Plains, New York. John and Aleatha were spending the weekend at the inn in celebration of their thirtieth wedding anniversary. Jude and Aleatha exchanged phone numbers, while John promised to bring his wife to Point Judith on their next vacation. "I would love to go deep sea fishing." Then John told David about his construction business and how he got started installing ponds. "I was surprised when I got the second call to install another pond right down the road. A year later, I had three more jobs lined up. I was so busy I had to buy another excavator," John said looking at his wife. "We've been together since high school," he said and then asked David how long he and Jude had been married. "Are the two of you celebrating an anniversary?"

David smiled. "No, we're celebrating life, enjoying every day together."

Jude looked at John and said, "David and I met in Point Judith a year ago. I was writing my new series and he offered to show me around." She touched the side of David's face with the back of her fingers tips. Then she looked at Aleatha. "I fell in love with him the moment I looked into his eyes. I knew he was the one I was waiting for."

"Aww, that's very romantic," Aleatha said and

reached out for John's hand. "Would the two of you care to go for a walk around the grounds? It stopped raining and I heard another guest say there's a koi pond on the other side of the garden shed."

The couples strolled discovering gorgeous garden beds, resting benches and yes the pond featuring large orange, white and spotted koi fish. The pond was surrounded by Japanese maples, ferns and several sedges. Jude took hold of David's hand telling Aleatha about the bear on their front porch. "Apparently, they love to eat the tender tips of the sedge grasses."

Aleatha told her about a bear knocking her bird feeder to the ground and destroying the planter below. "It was so bad, I thought a tornado went through the front yard," she said and then announced they had dinner reservations at her parent's house. "It was nice meeting you, I hope we get together again."

Jude gave her a warm hug and shook John's hand goodbye.

After they left David asked Jude if she wanted to go out for dinner that evening. "There's a nice restaurant right down the road called The Left Bank. They serve escargot." He stepped back so she couldn't get him, but when she nodded yes he said, "Okay, I'll make reservations for two at seven."

"I'd love that," she said, and he looked pleased as he kissed her on the cheek, and then reached for her hand to continue their garden tour.

At precisely six-thirty David stepped out of the bathroom ready to take her to dinner. He was wearing black slacks, and a black collarless shirt with neither a tie nor jacket. He was freshly shaven and looked like he just stepped out of the shower. She laughed as she made mention of her black summer dress. "Did you see me put on my leopard bra and panties?"

"You are an amazing woman, Jude," he whispered to her. "I never thought I would find someone I was so compatible with... until now," he added plaintively. "It's like you read my mind and know exactly what I am—"

She kissed him tenderly on the lips. "I wanted you to see them on the hanger in the bathroom."

"Great strategy romance writer, now I'll be sitting across for you undressing you the entire time."

She sashayed out the door and down the hall. When she lifted her dress ever so slightly he gasped. Then he ran up to her and swatted her on her derriere. "Your plan is to intentionally drive me crazy tonight is that it?"

David ordered the market oysters and when he heard Jude order the escargot he looked up from his menu.

She smiled at him and said the entire weekend was about discovering new things and trying something different. "I want to live life every day with you. I don't want to be afraid of anything." Then she looked up at their server and asked if she could have the Les Oeufs just in case.

"Of course you may have the deviled eggs. I'll bring enough for two."

David reach over and took her hand in his. "I'm so proud of you."

She squeezed his hand. "Until I met you I was afraid of everything. Water, people, even babies for heaven's sake." A lump formed in her throat. She smiled widely at him before telling him she hoped to spend the rest of her life with him. "I don't require expensive long weekends. As long as we are together, I'm happy."

"I like the idea of getting out of town every now and then. Besides, I want to discover so much with you. I really want to see you swallow that snail before he moves around in your mouth."

She threw her napkin at him. "You ass. Now I'm not eating them. You are."

David laughed so loud the woman sitting behind Jude turned around. "I'm sorry," he said and told the waiter to set the snails down in front of him and to give her another cocktail. Then what Jude did next was a total surprise to David. She scooped the snail out of the shell and ate it. Right before she finished both of their cocktails.

They were eating dinner when they overheard the waitress telling the bar tender about asking for a raise so he could afford the service dog for his son with autism. The man explained that even if he did get a raise it would take months if not years to save up the money. Jude reached over and tapped David on the hand.

David called the waitress over to the table. "I'm sorry we overheard you talking to the bar tender about needing a service dog for his son."

"Yeah, I'm sorry we're not supposed to talk about personal stuff when we're at work or we'll get fired. Please don't say anything."

"We won't," Jude said and asked how much a dog cost.

The woman saw the restaurant manager look her way and excused herself. "I'm sorry, I have to get back to work."

Jude looked at the manager and decided to take a chance on her being a decent human being. She put her napkin on the table and walked up to her. "Can I ask you something about one of your employees?"

"Of course," she said.

"Your bar tender seems like a nice guy."

"He is," she said adding, "He works hard, in fact, he's one of my best employees."

"He's a great bar tender," Jude said. "I was wondering if I could leave his tip with you."

"Sure," she replied.

"Great, I'll be right back." Jude went back to the table grabbed her cellphone and looked up the cost for a service dog. "It says anywhere from ten to twenty-thousand." Jude wrote the check for twenty-thousand-dollars. Got up and walked back over to the manager and asked what his name was, then she handed the check to her.

The woman had tears in her eyes. "Is this for what I think it is for?"

"Yes," Jude said. "For his son's service dog."

The woman hugged her and said she had to tell him so he could thank her. When she read the name on the check and said, "Wait. I read all of your books. I knew I recognized you."

"Aww, thank you and thank you for allowing me to do this." Jude's smile widened. "I'm learning the meaning of giving back." Then she walked over to the table and saw David. He was giving her two thumbs up.

When she sat down he asked her how it felt. "How do you feel right now?"

Jude blew out a breath. Sat down and replied, "Like I won the lottery." When she started to cry, David reached over and laced his gingers in hers.

Jude lifted her head and met his gaze. "Now I know why you are so generous."

David offered a goofy smile. "How did I get so lucky to find you?"

Jude leaned over the table and gave him a kiss, then squirmed in her chair playfully. "I'm so happy we found each other," she said. "I really am."

15

Monday afternoon, David and Jude were at the beach house when Jude got a call from her literary agent asking her when she would be returning to New York. She wanted to go over the year ahead and make plans for the new series. Jude told her she would have to get back to her. Jude's heart hammered her chest as she set her cellphone down. She turned to look out the window attempting to look his way, before she turned back around, David waved for her to come outside. The temperature was just right – not too hot, not too cold. The air was pleasant, with a gentle quality that felt soothing and refreshing, but Jude was shaking when she stepped out onto the patio.

David closed his laptop and asked her if she wanted to take a stroll down the beach. "It's almost dinner time, we can head down the beach and have a bite to eat at Aunt Carrie's."

Jude stood in front of him blinking rapidly as she seemed to fight back her tears and told him gently, "I don't want to leave you."

David nodded emphatically. He stood up and hugged her. Then he asked her, clearly trying to ease her emotions. "Why are you saying this? Did something happen?" His eyes wide waiting for her to answer him. He leaned back and looked into her eyes, pushed a smile across his face in an obvious attempt to ease her mind.

Jude offered an uneasy grin. "My lease is up."

"Okay," he replied. "We have two houses and..." David narrowed his eyes at her.

Jude was barely making eye contact with him when she said, "My life is in New York." Then as quick as her hand landed on his, it skittered away. Tears spilled down her cheeks.

David sensed something else was going on with her. He snapped his eyes shut as panic swelled within him and he let go of her other hand. When he pursed his lips in disappointment she looked down. David pulled out a chair for her to sit down. When she did, he sat down next to her and said, "Please talk to me."

Jude needed time to think. Never in her life had she ever been this perplexed. Then again, she never fell in love before either. "Would you get me a glass of water please?" She sat there thinking. *I don't drive because my publisher sends a car for me. In Point Judith, I will be without my agent, editor and my beloved publisher.* Her heart might not be able to take the loss. For twelve years they were her family. They treated her better than anyone ever did. She loved living in the city. *No matter how hard I try, I can't make the pieces fit together.* Jude thought about the weekend she and David just spent in Vermont. How it felt to be generous. She felt alive, invigorated and in love. David taught granted her the gift of giving and he showed her the meaning of true love. Tears trickled down her cheeks. Her heart was palpitating as she drew in a breath of salty air. The warmth of the sun felt good on her skin.

David handed her the glass, sat down in the chair next to her and when he caressed the top of her hand it all became clear to him. Jude was leaving. Fear swept over his face. He'd fallen in love her. In the distance someone was burning sage and he could hear music streaming from their radio. He watched as Jude wiped away her tears, sipped her water and shook her head before saying, "I have to go back to the city to meet with my literary agent and clear my head."

David's cellphone rang. They both looked down and saw the caller was Faith. "She'll leave a message," he said. "Jude, I love you."

"I know," she replied and told him that she loved him too. "Try to understand."

David sat stoic for a moment, then he got up and told her he would drive her back to the city. "When do you need to go back?"

"I." she hesitated for a minute knowing she had to clear all of her stuff out of the beach house and honor the contract by having the cleaning lady come back before she leaves. "I have to do a few things first. You don't have to drive me into the city, I can call my driver to come and get me."

David thought to himself. *So, this is it. She's leaving.*

Then Jude's cellphone rang. "It's Aunt Emily." She answered the call as David stood beside her. "Hello."

"Jude, I have wonderful news to share with you. Can you meet me in an hour?"

Jude looked up at David, but he was looking out at the ocean as if he were lost. She knew she upset him, but she also knew she had to be sure or what was it all for? She told Aunt Emily she was at David's beach house. "Do you want to see both David and me?" she asked.

"No, dear, just you. Let's meet at your beach house in an hour."

Jude set her phone down and told David, "I'm meeting Aunt Emily at my place in an hour. Are you okay?"

David turned around, gave her a hug and said he was going to the facility. "I have to go. Will you be here for dinner?"

A lump formed in her throat. She could see sadness on his face. Her bottom lip quivered as she said, "Yes and I'll cook."

No kiss goodbye, no pat on her derriere, he just turned and walked down the stairs. Jude sat on the porch curled up in a ball, crying. "I love him more than he knows. Oh, Lord, please. Why does this have to be so hard?" A few minutes later, she got up and walked down the beach toward her place. When she opened the door she was reminded as to why she rented the place in the first place. To write her stories.

Aunt Emily arrived in time to see Jude wiping away more tears. She hugged her and told her she may have answer to her problem.

When Aunt Emily heard about Judith Ann wanting to write a new beach series, she contacted Jude's previous editor to suggest he send her to Point Judith for a year. Then she got a hold of Grace to work her own magic on Jude.

Jude apologized to Aunt Emily and said she her heart hurt thinking about her career and about David. "I love him with all my heart, but I also love writing. Everyone is in the city. I need to be." She stopped herself. "I'm sorry, you wanted to talk to me about something and here I am going on and on about poor Jude."

"How about we sit down with a nice cup of tea and a blueberry scones?" Aunt Emily reached in her bag and took out a container of scones and tin of lemon tea.

While Aunt Emily set the table Jude put on a kettle of water. Aunt Emily laughed as Jude tied her hair up in a high ponytail declaring it was getting hot.

"Summer, is coming way too soon for my blood," Jude said and poured hot water in their cups. Then she took a bite of her scones. Inhaled once, closed her eyes and smiled. "So good."

"Jude, how would you feel if I purchased your penthouse along with my friend Geraldine and allowed you to stay there whenever you had business to tend to?"

Jude's face lit up, her heart came back to life. "Seriously?"

"Yes, Geraldine and I both have business in the city and on occasion we both like to go there for events. We would also like to use the apartment for overnight stays when we are traveling to and from the airports."

Jude knew what Aunt Emily was doing. Her matchmaking just got real. She was flattered. "My editor said we could use Zoom for our monthly meetings and my literary agent did say she would love to spend time at the beach whenever we had to—"

"So, that's a yes? You'll sell it to us and move to Point Judith?" Aunt Emily raised her eyebrows.

Jude cried happy tears. "Aunt Emily, I accept your offer and just so you know. I have not only fallen in love with your nephew, I plan on spending the rest of my life making him happy." She jumped up and clapped her hands. "You have no idea how hard this was for me. My life was in New York, but my heart lives here. I love David and I promise you I will make him a good wife." Her words lingered for a moment. Her hand went to her mouth and she cried. Aunt Emily got up and hugged her.

"And he will be the best husband to you. The two of you were made for one another." She scrunched her nose. "He doesn't really care for children either."

Jude wondered how she knew that about her. "I never wanted to have kids. I guess I just love my job too much, but yea David and I talked about not having children. We both get so much more out of helping strangers." Jude told Aunt Emily about the children's hospital and about the single dad and his son's autism.

"I am proud of the two of you. Jude, you just made me the happiest woman in the world."

16

April 30th, Jude left the keys to the beach house on the kitchen counter, paid the maid service to do one final sweep of the house and then emailed a thank you letter to the realtor for finding the house at the last minute. She stepped outside and smiled, taking in one last scent of the ocean's breeze, before locking the back door. She had one hour to say goodbye to David before the car service arrived to take her back to the city. Before she tied the ivory sweater over her shoulders, she bent down and picked up a piece of sea glass someone must have dropped at the front door. Jude tied the sweater into a knot, picked up her luggage and slowly walked down to David's. She set her luggage down on his front porch and rang the doorbell. David opened the door holding eleven pieces of sea glass. "I was going to give you these this morning, but your light wasn't on." He raised his shoulders, telling her, "I had twelve, I must have dropped one along the way."

Jude smiled and held up the twelfth piece. "This one?" Then she stepped inside. "I found it at my back door. I went outside to get one more look at the ocean." She stood on her tippy toes and kissed him.

"I made coffee and Aunt Emily sent over your favorite chocolate scones, along with a basket filled with snacks for you to take." He closed the door and held his hand out for her to go to the kitchen.

"I love Aunt Emily," she said and took the sweater off. When she approached the counter, she set the sweater down on the back of a chair. Then she picked up a scone and took a bite.

David handed her a small plate and her coffee. "I think she loves you more."

Jude studied his face. She knew what he was saying, but he was wrong. Her love for Aunt Emily was stronger than he could imagine and, she loved him.

They both heard her cellphone ping. The driver was outside waiting for her. "My driver is here." She stood up and held her hands out for a hug. David wrapped his arms around her, leaned in and kissed her tenderly. Jude leaned back and said, "I'll call you as soon as I get home."

David swallowed the lump in his throat, held back his tears and nodded before kissing her one last time. An hour later, he picked up her sweater, inhaled her scent and wept.

A week had gone by and David was refusing to accept the fact that she was not by his side. On Saturday, Aunt Emily showed up unannounced. "Good morning," David said as he met her in the foyer.

She looked at him and her heart broke. "You need to be faithful and trust God. David, she—"

"She's gone. Aunt Emily, I tried. I promised to love her until the day I died. I'm not moving to New York."

Aunt Emily noticed the ivory sweater on the back of the kitchen stool. "I see you've moved on," she said and pointed toward the kitchen.

David looked at her and then at then at the sweater. "It's Jude's, she forgot it." He walked over, picked it up and asked her if she would mail it to Jude. "I know I should have—"

Aunt Emily took the sweater from his grip and set it back down. "I'm sorry things didn't work out for the two of you. I honestly thought she was the one for you."

David nodded in agreement. "So did I." Then he shrugged his shoulders. "I had to let her go. Her life is in New York. If she loves me as I do her—"

"Then she will be back," Aunt Emily said, looking at the sweater one last time.

It only took two weeks to close on the property.

Geraldine Prescott said she loved every aspect of it and she offered to buy the Gustav Klimt painting of Freya's Tears. "This is marvelous," Geraldine said as she accepted the keys from Jude. "How well Grace knows me," she said and gave Jude one of her own business cards. "If you ever change your mind." She pointed toward the front door. "That door will always be open."

"Wait, did you say Grace. The same Grace that rented the beach house to me? Mrs. Sammon? Then they both laughed aloud. Jude reached out and touched Geraldine's hand and said, "I plan on living my best life with the love of my life and that means I will be leaving this city in my rearview mirror."

Jude gave the U-Haul driver the directions one more time and said she would see them in a little while, then she got in her car and told her driver, "Take me home, please."

Two hours later, David sat on the bottom step holding the sweater in his hands waiting for the love of his life to drive up any minute. His heart started beating faster when she stepped out of the car. Jude ran into his open arms, cried, "I love you so much and yes, you, salty beast I have fallen in love with Point Judith."

David hugged her tighter. "I love you more than you know. I promise to make every day a day to remember." He winked at her. "Starting with today. Then he got down on one knee, and said, "Will you marry me?"

Jude's driver set her luggage down on the bottom

step and slowly clapped his hands. Jude's eyes filled with tears. She reached down and cupped David's face in her hands and said, "Yes, my love, I will marry you." Then she smiled warmly at her driver as he tapped her on her shoulder and waved goodbye for the last time.

17

David picked Jude up and carried her inside. Once he closed the door, she cried the happiest of tears. After David opened a bottle of champagne Jude told him, "Those were the hardest days of my life."

He poured their champagne and asked, "What are you talking about? Your tour?"

She walked up to him and gave him a squeeze. "No, being away from you."

After they toasted to their future, they made each other a promise to always share their dreams and heart's desires with one another. Jude told David she wanted a small intimate ceremony. Then she brushed her hand under his chin. "Can we get married at Aunt Emily's, please?"

David smiled and told her, "That will make her and me very happy."

Jude clapped her hands. "Umm, me too. I love her house. Let's call her, I'll put her on speakerphone," she said and dialed her number. Jude didn't wait for David to tell her. She shouted, "We're getting married."

"Congratulations! Oh, David, I am so happy for you. Jude, I feel blessed to have you as my niece. Welcome to the family, dear. Am I allowed to share the news?" she asked as she motioned for Maria to come closer.

"Of course," Jude said and David nodded in agreement.

"David and Jude are getting married."

When Jude and David heard Maria praying for them, they hugged each other. David told Aunt Emily they would be stopping by to talk to her after the weekend.

Jude held the phone closer to her mouth and said, "Wait until you see my ring. It's gorgeous."

"Oh, this is wonderful news. I'm so excited I can't stand it. I love you both. Okay, I have to make a few calls. Bye."

David told Jude he wasn't sharing her with anyone for the next three days. "Where would you like to go and don't say the cabin. This is a special occasion."

She pouted her lips and held her hands in a prayer like pose. "Do it for me. It's my happy place."

"Do you know how long I waited for a woman like

you?" he replied and kissed her. "I have one more surprise for you."

She capped her hands. "I love surprises. Hey, instead of the cabin can we take the Bill Pay out? I want to spend our summers at the cabin and winters at the beach house." She scrunched her nose. "No kids, right?"

David opened his briefcase and pulled out a file folder. He set the listings on the counter and said, "I thought about your idea of being able to write with no distractions." He twisted his mouth and smiled adding, "And no kids." Then he held his hands in the air. "It's totally up to you, but I thought we deserved our own place. Somewhere we can live and make new memories."

"God I hope this isn't menopause," she said as she wiped away more tears. "David, every day with you is like a new and brighter ray of sunshine." She shook her head. "I can't believe I'm so emotional."

"I wanted to give you options."

"Options," she said and picked up the first listing.

David pulled out a second folder. That folder had over twenty listings in it. Then he picked the pile up and said, "Or, we can shop for new home together."

Jude gazed deeply into his eyes. Then she looked at the houses and asked, "Which one do you like the best?"

David tilted his head to the left and took in a deep breath before saying, "Care to guess?"

Jude held her finger to her lips, grabbed the listings

and sat at the counter looking at every document. When she pointed to the brick house with the black security gate, he nodded. Then he called Grace and said, "She picked it and by the way, she said yes."

Jude held her hand out for his phone and told Grace, "Thank you. They are all nice, but this one has our name on it. When can we see it?"

Grace cleared her throat and said, "Today. Write this down." Then she gave Jude the code to the gate and told her the combination to the lockbox. "I'm so happy for the two of you and Jude, I cried when Aunt Emily told me the two of you were getting married."

Jude reached out for David's hand. "So, Mrs. Grace Sammon, you were the real estate agent behind all of my transactions."

"Shut up," Grace replied. "How did you figure it out?"

"Hahaha, well, Mrs. Sammon, your friend, Geraldine slipped.

Grace laughed aloud. "I love you guys. Enjoy the home tour." She went to hang up but stopped. "Jude, David saved me when I was in a really dark place. He's like a brother to me and if it's okay with you, I'd like to be your new sister-in-law."

Jude smiled from ear to ear. "Absolutely. I love the idea of having a little sister. When will the baby be here? We would like to visit."

"Oh, gosh. August," Grace said and then announced she had to go. "This momma has to pee."

Jude laughed. "Bye hot momma."

Jude held up the paper and said, "Grace said we can go now?"

David set his glass on the counter and pointed for the door. "Just so you know, I wanted to wait for you before I toured any of them." Then he held the door open for her. "Jude, you can look online if Grace's list isn't what you're looking for."

Jude got in the Tahoe and told David, "I can't believe we both chose the same house. Let's look and see if it meets our needs." Jude could feel David's excitement.

David pulled up to the gate and Jude gave him the code. The driveway was lined with stone pavers in shades of gray and slate blue. The bespoken estate was in a prestigious neighborhood. From the hardwood floors to the custom tile in the foyer the home breathed world-class. "David, this is definitely a lifestyle of luxury and distinction. Wow."

David closed the door and laughed. "Imagine the memories we can make in this home. And we are just minutes from Aunt Emily." He put his hands on her shoulders. "Let's check out the rest of the home. David walked up to the fireplace in the living room and said, "The stone is the same as the stone on the outside. I like it."

Jude looked at it. "It's not as big as the fireplace at the cabin."

Next, they went into the office. "This room has your name on it," he said.

"No way, who puts a soaking tub in the corner." Jude said as she walked past the first bathroom.

"It has a wine cellar," he said as he held his hand out for her to enter the kitchen.

He laughed when she reminded him they both drank beer.

"This is gorgeous," she said when she saw the master bedroom ensuite and the walk-in closet.

"I like the fireplace at the end of the bed," he said and touched her elbow as he walked toward the kitchen.

"That's nice," Jude said as she opened the sauna door.

The kitchen offered white cabinets, stainless steel appliances and a marble counter, everything they both hated. "David, I love our cabin. We don't need another house. I'm content with what we have." She lifted herself up onto the counter and used her pointer finger to call him closer to her. She rested her hands on his shoulders. "I can't shake the feeling I experienced when we were in Vermont." She shook her head ever so slightly. Kissed his lips and looked into his eyes. "My heart still skips a beat thinking about helping that young man and his son." She tapped his nose. "You taught me the meaning of love and how to be grateful for what we have. I would rather live in the cabin and be able to help others than live in this fancy house."

He kissed her on the forehead. Held her tight in his arms. Leaned back and told her, "I love you Mrs. Wayne and together we are going to live our best lives." Then he picked her up and took her outside to see the swimming pool and pointed to the ocean.

"Wow, I had no idea we were that close. It's nice." She inhaled the salty air and waved her hand at him. "Our ocean view is way better," she laughingly said. "Come on, let's go home."

David and Jude climbed aboard the Bill Pay where they spent the next three days, laughing and making plans for their wedding, honeymoon. They were sitting topside on the chase lounge. Jude sat between his legs with her head resting on his chest. "I was thinking about asking my literary agent to stand up for me."

"That sounds nice. How do you feel about me asking Grace to stand next to me?"

Jude looked up at him. "She would be honored and I love the idea."

David kissed the top of her head. "Since I have been everywhere, care to tell me where you would like to go on our honeymoon?"

"Well, I've always wanted to go to Bali," she replied and reached for her beer. When she took a sip she declared it was warm. "We need cold beers." She sat up and turned to face him. "I'll grab two more while you think about where you want to go."

When she came back he told her he always wanted to go to Lombok. "Lombok?" she said and handed him his beer.

He took a sip and told her, "It's an island in Indonesia." Then he grabbed his cellphone and showed her a few pictures.

"Pink sand, turquoise water and a whole lot of tranquility." Jude tapped her beer to his. "You win. Indonesia here we come."

"How about both," he replied and emptied his bottle. "I would love to show you around Bali first and then we can discover Lombok for the first time, together."

Jude clapped her hands as her smile widened. "I want to stop at the gift store on the way home. I'm going to start a journal and write down all of our adventures."

He reached for her to come closer. "And when we are old and gray we'll sit back and rediscover every tantalizing detail."

"Oh, the memories we shall make," she said and rested her head on his lap.

race was so happy for David and Jude. She ran into the living room and told Steve the news. "Oh, my goodness, it worked. David asked Jude to marry him and she said yes." Grace clapped her hands and then held them in a prayer like position. "I'm so excited. He's such a good person, he deserves happiness and to be in love."

Steve patted his knee and when Grace sat down he told her he hoped they had a dozen children together. "I'm so glad he found someone." Then they heard the kids coming in the backdoor.

Grace kissed Steve and announced, "It's dinnertime." When she got up she felt the baby kick. Grace stood there for a minute waiting and when she took Steve's hand and rested it on her belly, he felt his child move for the first time.

"She's a kicker," he said and smiled.

"What if she is a boy?" Grace said as they walked out to the kitchen. "Who's hungry?"

All three children raised their hands. Maddie began setting the table, while Mal and Hudson poured iced tea in everyone's glasses. Grace took the potato salad out of the fridge and then handed Steve the platter filed with hamburgers and hot dogs. "Maddie grab the buns please?" Steve called out to her as he held the back door open. When she asked Grace if she was okay, Steve set the platter down on the counter and quickly made his way to Grace. "Grace, what's wrong?"

She was holding onto the counter, tears building in her eyes. Her face was flushed. Hudson, Mal and Maddie stood in front of her, holding onto each other. "Mom," Maddie said and she too started to cry. "Mom," Maddie called out again then looked at her father. "Dad, is she okay? Is the baby coming?"

Steve put his hand on Grace's shoulder. "Sweetheart, what's wrong?"

"I'm okay kids. I'm just happy," she cried and everyone started breathing again. "I'm sorry, I didn't mean to scare everyone," Grace laughingly cried.

The kids proceeded to bring everything out to the patio, while Steve hugged Grace. Pulled himself back, looking stunned before regaining his composure. "Don't do that to me. To us. What are you crying about?"

"I'm so happy. I have you, the kids and my two best

friends. And David is getting married. You have no idea how happy that makes me." She laughed and reached for a tissue. "Everyone tried to fix us up, but he truly is a brother from another mother to me and I'm happy he found Jude."

Steve rubbed his finger over her smiling lips. "He's a great guy that's for sure." His eyebrows scrunched together, then he barked out a laugh. "No more shocks. Okay, I'm going out to fire up the grill. Are you sure you're okay?"

She waved him off. "I'm fine. I want to call Ava and tell her the news." Then she dialed her number. "Huh, no answer. Maybe, she eloped. No, she wouldn't dare. Would she?" Grace called Shelby's phone. Same thing. It went straight to voicemail. "What the hell!"

"Mommy, you said a bad word," Hudson said as he grabbed the grilling utensil for Steve.

Grace laughed as her son went out the door shaking his head. A minute later, her cellphone rang. "Ava, where are you?"

"We're in New Mexico," she replied and Grace heard Shelby tell her to say hi.

"Oh, okay. Anyway, I have good news. David and Jude are getting married." Grace pulled the phone away from her ear when both Shelby and Ava shouted yahoo.

"Isn't that great news?" Grace said. Silence. "Hello, did I lose you?"

"Grace, Shelby and I got married last night. Grace? Oh, Jesus. Grace," Ava shouted.

"I'm here. I'm happy for you. Please tell Shelby congratulations."

"Are you okay? I was going to tell you, but we wanted to—"

Grace interrupted her. "Ava, I love you and I am happy for the two of you. Seriously, it's all good. Please have a drink on me. Now go enjoy your honeymoon. We'll talk when you get home. God, that sounds so nice to say. I love you Ava."

"And I love you, Grace. Shelby sends her love. We'll see you next week. Bye."

"Bye," Grace said and put her cellphone down. She sat at the counter feeling pure joy. Her heart was full. All her dreams were coming true. She decided not to call Ella. She went outside and saw her family playing catch in the backyard as they wait for the burgers to cook. Grace sat down in the lawn chair and smiled. When Steve turned and saw her sitting there smiling at the children, he shared smile.

The next day was Sunday and Ella had invited them to take a tour of her new property. She wanted to show Grace and Steve where the house was going. When they pulled up to the empty lot, Brody pulling the for sale sign out of the ground.

With her arm wrapped around Grace, Ella showed her where the house would be built then she heard

Brody telling Steve about his three bay garage. Grace looked at Ella. "What?" Ella said offering a coy smile.

"You're pregnant," Grace whispered. Then pointed to her swollen belly.

"Hahaha, I wish," Ella said and pointed towards Brody. "It's his fault. He eats mashed potatoes and macaroni salad and ice cream every night." Then she brushed her belly in a downward motion. "I didn't gain that much weight."

19

Emily and Geraldine exited the taxi and got a true glimpse of New York during the early summer months as they both took their first breath of city air that day. There was a slight breeze in the air, but beneath it all the humidity hit them full force, their hair was beginning to stick to the back of their necks. NYC felt more like July then it did the last day of May. Geraldine reached into her bag and pulled out her sunglasses as Emily paid their driver. The doorman immediately recognized them and offered to assist them inside the building. "I must have been out of my mind to allow you to convince me to buy in this godforsaken jungle," Geraldine says as she steps inside the elevator.

"Oh, stop. What do you want to do? Sell the damn place. Forget I ever said that. We are not selling it. What if Jude needs to use the apartment? We have to hold onto it until they get married." Emily held the door open for her. "You're such a queen." Then she waved her off.

"It's bribery," Geraldine says as she plops into a chair. "Never mind the taxi didn't have air conditioning, oh no, we have to come when it's almost a hundred degrees outside." She stands up and smiles when she sees Emily pouring them each a cocktail. First, she kicked off her shoes then she fanned herself. "Bless your heart," she says as she accepts the cosmopolitan. "Well, at least the apartment comes with a fully stocked bar." She takes a sip and squeezes a fresh lime in her glass. Then she holds it up in mock toast. "To David and Jude, may they get married soon, very soon."

Emily's cellphone rang. "Speak of the devil. It's David. Hello, dear," she says and sits down on the sofa sipping her cocktail as she listened to David tell they want to know if they could get married at her home in July. Emily holds up her thumb and replies, "July sounds wonderful."

Geraldine claps her hands and refills both of their glasses. "Praise, God."

Emily waves her off and tells David she is in the city with Geraldine for the next few days. "We're going to see a play and have dinner with a friend of ours." When she sets her cellphone down she tells Geraldine, "We have a wedding to plan."

David was standing in the kitchen when Jude walked up to him. "I couldn't wait, I called Aunt Emily and told her we wanted to get married at her house in July."

Jude tilted her head, pursed her lips and said, "This July, right?" Then she walked up to him, kissed him and forced him to walk backwards to the living room. When she pushed him down on the sofa he grinned up at her. Jude slowly took off her clothes and sat on David's lap. Five minutes later, they heard Marie come through the front door. David moved Jude to the other end of the sofa and lie down on top of her.

He held his finger to his lips then whispered in her ear, "She'll set the grocery bags down on the counter, put the dairy in the fridge and go straight to the laundry room. When she does, I'm making a beeline for the bedroom."

Jude laughed at the thought. David immediately put his hand over her mouth. "Shhh," he whispered in her ear and they both giggled.

When Marie answered her cellphone, David and Jude both raised their eyebrows. They listened as she told Aunt Emily she would be glad to help serve at David and Jude's wedding. "Of course, Miss Emily, yes I am so excited too. No, they are both out. Okay, I will see you tomorrow," she said and walked toward the laundry room, but when she stopped in the foyer both Jude and David slid down onto the floor. Maria opened the door and grabbed the mail out of the mailbox, set it on the counter and then went to the laundry room.

David held his hand out for Jude to get up and then ran to his bedroom. Jude collapsed onto the bed laughing. "That was close."

David moved closer to her and said, "I was done. Care to finish what you started?"

"Umm, no." she pointed toward the door. "What if she comes in for the sheets and towels?"

David shook his head. "She never comes through a closed door."

Jude gave him a seductive smile and pointed toward the shower. When they stepped out of the bedroom Maria was upstairs cleaning David's office. He called out for her to let her know they were in the house. "Good morning, Maria."

"Morning David," she replied from the top of the stairs. Then she made her way down to the kitchen. "Oh, Jude, congratulations." Maria gave them both a hug. "I am so happy for you."

Jude kissed her on the cheek and thanked her. "I am so blessed to have all of you in my life. "Thank you so much for all that you do for us."

"I love taking care of my clients, especially Emily and David." She reached over and touched the side of Jude's face before adding, "Now, I get to take of you."

David hugged her and told Jude, "Maria has been taking care of me since I was fourteen." He winked at her adding, "She taught me how to make a proper bed, how to navigate around Point Judith and how to change a tire."

"Yes, and you taught me the importance of saving money for my future." She patted Jude's hand, "I have a very nice retirement plan thanks to David."

David kissed her on the forehead and told her they were going to the new living facility to greet a few new residents. "We'll see you on Monday," he said and picked up his baseball cap.

In the car, Jude asked David, "Can I share something with you?"

"Anything," he said and waited for her to tell him what was on her mind before he put the car in drive.

Jude put her seatbelt on and held David's right hand in her own. "This is the first time in my life that I didn't have to worry." She brought his hand to her lips and kissed his fingertips.

David put the car in reverse, backed out of the driveway and drove toward Ocean Road. "I'll always be here for you, take care of you and make sure all your dreams come true, Jude." He turned toward her before heading onto the highway. "I love you with all my heart."

Jude rested their hands on the center console. "when I was a little girl, I worried about my father a lot, as a teenager, I was concerned about my mother's health and then when I moved to the city, that I hated, I worried I made the wrong move, but I did what I had to make myself fit in. I'm grateful to everyone who helped my writing journey." She inhaled a deep breath adding, "When I am with you, I feel safe."

David went to say something, but Jude cut him off and his gaze lingered.

"David, I don't need a bigger house, a fancy car or expensive clothes. You—" she stared to cry but stopped herself. She took back her hand and wiped her eyes. "Your love is all I need." She looked at him. "I love you and I can't wait to be your wife."

David stopped at for the red light, leaned over and hugged her before telling her, "I will always keep you safe." He was almost to the facility when he said, "Thank you for choosing us." He laughed. "I knew you couldn't escape the spell of Point Judith."

"Yeah, that's some spell you all casted on me. Ocean views, fresh salty air in the morning, never mind watching you jog past my window every morning."

When they pulled up to the facility they saw the van and bus unloading men and women. Faith waved to them as David parked the Tahoe. "Wow," Jude said. "Can I hire her to be my personal assistant?"

David laughed. "You have Aunt Emily's entire entourage and now you want mine. She would love it," he said and opened the door to get out.

"She's so efficient," Jude said and waved to Faith. "Good morning, Faith."

"Good morning." She pointed to the greeting table

under the big tent. "It's tour day." Then she clapped her hands. "David, I have someone for you to meet." She took hold of his elbow and walked over to the rear of the tent. Two ladies were sitting behind a table asking guests what activities they enjoyed. "Barbara, Mary, this id David Wayne and his girlfriend, Jude."

"Fiancé," David said and then held his hand out to the ladies. "Ladies, I'd like to introduce the two of you to the future Mrs. Wayne."

One woman shook Jude's hand, the other said, "There goes my shot. Oh, honey, congratulations."

"Thank you," Jude said and asked what they were up to. "What are the two of you working on?"

"We are registering everyone for the activity club," Barbara said and Mary nodded in agreement.

"We both used to run the senior center until our husband's past away," Mary said and winked at David. "She's gorgeous. You better take care of her."

"Thank you," David replied adding, "She's a treasure."

Faith winked at Jude. "Is he ready?"

"I think so," Jude replied and touched David's elbow. "I think they're ready for you."

David appeared surprised almost shocked. "Today's the day," he said and moved toward the microphone. When he stepped closer to the front of the crowd he saw Amelia sitting next to a group of men and women. He waved to her and to several of the merchants. "First, I would like to say thank you to everyone. Wow, it's not even our grand opening and you're all here. Thank you." Then he motioned for Jude and Faith to come up. He held their hands, raised them in the air and said, "Ladies and gentlemen I would like to introduce you to my fiancé Jude and to the woman behind all of this. Faith. I am the luckiest man alive. None of this would have been possible if not for their help and all of you."

Jude whispered, "Grace, you should mention her."

David shook his head. "Man, she's right. Jude reminded me about one other woman. The woman who found this piece of property and believed I could do all of this. I promise you she will be here for the grand opening. Shall we take our first tour of the place?"

Tour day was a success. All of the merchants were there to greet the residents and to offer samples of their goods. At the end of the tour, Amelia approached David with another donation. This one was from the group of doctors tagged along with her. Amelia introduced David and Jude to the nurses and doctors before giving him the check for over one million dollars. "This is for the new clinic," she said.

One of the nurses told David that she was touched by his generosity and had to be a part of it all. "When I heard about your kindness to Amelia's father and about all of this, I knew I wanted to do something." She offered a sheepish grin. "My father was a Vietnam veteran. He would have wanted to be a part of it as well, but he passed away a month ago. When I saw he left me everything, I told Amelia I wanted in." Then she handed David a separate check. "Please accept this on behalf of my father." When she looked at Jude and saw her crying, the woman broke down in her own tears. David hugged her.

"Thank you so much," he said and held her by the shoulders. "I promise you and your father, I will make sure everyone here knows where this money came from." Then he told them why he named the facility Rhode Island Red.

Amelia and Jude hugged each other listening to David speak about one of the greatest men he had ever met. "Like so many disabled, veterans, and homeless people Red was an exceptional human being. Red taught me the meaning of taking care of others in a quiet manner. These men and women deserve to be treated with kindness and respect."

Several of the doctors shook David's hand, telling him there should be more places like this. "I hope this is just the beginning and more people are inspired by your generosity and vision."

Amelia promised David they would all be back for the grand opening. "We're so excited. Seriously, the people are lovely and everyone is so appreciative."

David hugged her. "I hope Red is watching over—"

"Oh, he is," Amelia replied and waved goodbye to Faith. "Bye, Jude and congratulations."

"Thank you," Jude replied and gave her a hug good-bye. Then she walked the entire grounds listening to Faith talk about each vendor, tenant and everything special about the facility.

Faith stopped outside the recreation room, smiled at them and said, "Your gift arrived and the men love it." She opened the door and four men were shooting pool, listening to Willie Nelson singing, "On The Road Again."

"Hey," they said as David entered.

David shook their hands and introduce Jude to them. Jude smiled when she saw a woman carrying a tray of snacks out from the kitchen. "Can I help you," Jude asked and the woman's smile spread slowly.

"Some habits are hard to break. I waited on my husband all the time. Unlike the bastard who left me for a crack whore, these guys know how to treat a woman. They even thank me for making their lunch."

Jude laughed, look back at David and said, "I'll swat him upside the head if he ever leaves me for any damn women."

20

At three-thirty, David and Jude returned back to the beach house. David laughingly said, "Yes, Jude, we can go back up to the cabin."

Jude walked out onto the back porch and saw children playing in the sand, couples lying on blankets, people were riding waves, while a few played volleyball. She watched the action. The sun was hotter than a firecracker, and she thought, unlike the city everyone looks happy. "David, I think it's time you and I take a dip in the ocean."

He looked back at her surprised by her words. His gaze was on her as if he had been waiting for that moment all his life. She shrugged her shoulders as if she was unable to process his silence. He continued to look at her for a long moment. When Jude turned to go inside, he followed her into the bedroom where she put on her one piece swim suit. David put his swim wear on as well. Hand in hand, they walked down to the beach. Side by side, not speaking. Jude smiled up at him before entering the water. Then she surprised herself by taking the plunge. She exhaled a long breath. David nodded cheerfully and gave a little snort that may have been in agreement or disagreement. Jude muttered, "Come on. It's refreshing."

David swam out to her.

"This is my new happy place," she teased. "Look at those sailboats."

David turned around and saw a row of them heading into the sun. "Sun catchers," he said and held his hands out to her. A gaze swept across his face as she made her way toward him. "You're my happy place. Whenever I am with you, I am happy. Promise me—"

She straddled her legs around his waist and lean back. David swung her in a full circle. Then he picked her up and held her in his arms. "I promise not to leave you for a crack whore." He laughed so hard she started laughing.

"That woman was serious. She said her husband would not allow her to work outside the home because it was embarrassing to him. So when he left her, she had no choice but to go on welfare. Let's just say they only provide the basic physical and material items needed for a person's well-being. They literally handed her a cane and a block of cheese at her first visit. What?" Jude looked into David's eyes and started laughing even harder. "Oh, my goodness, David. I have to buy a dress. I'm getting married."

"Hey, I'm getting married too. Just make sure your dress matches my Bermuda shorts." He waited for her to object, but when she nodded, he knew she was the one. "Seriously?'

"Oh, hell yeah. In fact, I'm not even wearing shoes. It's our wedding. We can go naked if we want."

"Okay, now you're just making fun of me," he said and swam toward the shore.

She called out to him. "I'm serious. Okay, I'll put on a sun dress. But no shoes." Jude swam up next to him. Can we invite everyone from Connecticut?"

"You can invite whomever you want. I'm sure Aunt Emily has the entire menu planned and the linens. You may want to let her know your preferences."

"David, Emily Marshall is hosting my wedding. She can do whatever she wants." She smiled. "Okay, our wedding. Let's go shopping. Can my dress match your shorts?"

"Mrs. Wayne, I think we should call Ava and ask her to make your dress and my shorts."

"Great idea," Jude said and handed him a towel. They sat on the beach and watched as the sun slowly headed for the other end of the water. "It's so beautiful and relaxing here." She put her head on his chest as three little boys ran past kicking up sand everywhere.

Jude grabbed a handful of sand and tossed it their way. "Okay, you're kidding about matching dress and shorts, right?"

David laughed hysterically. "Can you imagine the looks on their faces?"

She looked at him trying to figure out what in the world he just said. "What?" She shook her head at him. "I'm hungry. Let's go to George's and sit topside."

"Woman after my own heart. Shower first. I'll race you," he said and wrapped his towel around her feet before bolting up the stairs.

Once in the shower, they both agreed her dress had to be kept a secret. "I want to look into your eyes that day and be surprised."

"I can't wait to walk toward you. Just knowing we are going to spend the rest of our lives together. Living our best life."

"You're definitely a writer," he teased. "Hey, when are you going to start writing again?"

"Funny you should ask. I left my laptop up at the cabin."

"So, we're going to the cabin tonight?"

"Nope," she said and turned to allow the water to rinse her hair. "I'm going with you to the facility to finish putting the supplies in the closets and make the beds. And on Monday, we are going to greet our final home owner."

"It really did fill up fast," David replied as he got out

of the shower. Hand in hand, they strolled to the restaurant taking in the floral scents. As they walked past the wild roses, Jude noticed David became extremely quiet.

The hydrangeas near George's offered a pleasant honey-vanilla smell that made you want to stop and inhale. "Don't they smell good," she asked and then asked him what he was going to order. Jude furrowed her brow. "David, hello. Earth to David."

"I'm sorry. Did you say something?" He stopped to open the door for her.

She blinked a few times before answering him. "I asked you what you were going to order. Are you okay?"

David raised an eyebrow at the hostess and pointed toward the stairs. "Topside, please." Then he put his hand on Jude's back and followed her up the steps. When he held the chair out for her, he said he was thinking about all the people who were still living in the shelters. "What about the others?"

Their server came to the table and took their drink order along with their choice of appetizers.

Jude told him, "Let's take the twelve million you were going to spend on the estate and build another site." She raised her eyebrows.

David noticed a man sitting at the bar glance back when Jude said that. Their server set their drinks down and their order of clams.

Jude held her bottle up and tapped David's. "To our

next project. May there be no homeless people in the entire state."

"Here, here," David said and helped himself to a clam.

A moment later, their server came back to the table and took their dinner order. David ordered the seafood pot pie and Jude got the baked stuffed shrimp. "Can I get a bloody mary with my dinner please?"

"Make that two," David said.

When they finished eating, David noticed the man got up the same time they did. He wondered if the guy was interested in the living facility. Several times during the evening the man turned and looked at them. Perhaps, he was a veteran. His was wearing a Harley Davidson T-shirt, jeans and nice black leather boots. David offered his hand to him and said, "By any chance did you serve in Vietnam?"

The man looked at David like he had three heads. "Why do ask?" he said in a gruff tone.

David sensed he hit a nerve. "I thought I recognized you. My fault." Then he took Jude by the hand and left.

When Jude and David went down the stairs, the guy asked the bartender, "Who hell was that?"

"Huh," the bartender replied. "That was David Wayne, one of the richest, nicest guys you will ever meet. What'd he say to you?"

The guy turned around without answering.

Outside, Jude asked David he knew that man. "Is he a friend of yours?"

"No, I thought he wanted to say something, but I guess I was wrong." Then he pointed to across the street. "Care to sit outside and listen to the band for a while?" Chaplin's was serving buy one beer on tap and get the second one free. Under the gazebo, people sat all around the bar sipping their cocktails and listening to the music. David and Jude sat at one of the picnic tables. "We'll have two glasses of Michelob and a basket of fried oysters," David said as the waitress lit their candle.

Jude whispered in his ear. "Someone is hungry."

David shook his head. "You have to eat something or they risk losing their liquor license. Rhode Island rules." Then he winked at her. "We can take them home. I could eat the damn things for breakfast, their so sweet."

By the time they finished their second beer, they both cleared their plates. "That was so good," Jude declared and watched as the band came back from their break.

Then they heard the singer say it was time for karaoke. "Okay, the first song requires one guy and one gal. Do we have any takers?"

David smiled when he saw Jude read the sign hanging over the bar, karaoke night.

"Seriously," she said and smiled.

A tall husky man sitting at one of the other picnic tables shouted, "What's the song?"

The singer called out to him, "Shallow." And Jude's eyes lit up.

When she raised her hand in the air, David snapped his chin back. "I'm not singing, so forget about it."

The singer pointed to the guy. "You ready?" Then he pointed to Jude.

The crowd roared when the guy sang in a deep, gravelly and the exact amount of raspy in his voice as Bradley Cooper. Jude's eyes opened wide and when she sang, "Tell me something boy aren't you tired trying to fill that void?" David was on his feet cheering her on. At the end of the song, Jude and her singing partner received a standing ovation from the crowd.

"More," someone shouted and the DJ told them the next song was perfect for them.

"Care to give Picture a try?" Jude's singing partner asked.

Jude shrugged her shoulders and replied, "Sure."

Jude sang every word looking right at David and when the song was over she blew him a kiss, took her bow and thanked her singing partner. "That was amazing. You're really good," she said and gave him a slight hug. The bartender sent over free beers to both of their tables.

David slowly clapped as Jude approached the table. "Wow where did that come from?"

She drank for her plastic cup nearly emptying it.

"Ahh," then she sat down and said, "Four years of chorus."

"You were amazing Jude." David nodded his head. "Bravo." When he saw her look at the empty basket where the fried oysters were, he reached over and held her hand in his. "Are you still hungry?"

She bit the inside of her cheek. "Hmmm, did you make ice cream today?"

He laughed aloud. "We have the brandied cherry and I think a little bit of the mint chocolate chip left."

She shook her head and drew her lips in a flat line. "I ate that yesterday, but the cherry sounds delicious."

David grabbed their cups and empty basket in time to hand everything to the waitress. "Thank you," he said as he handed everything to her.

She smiled at Jude. "You're the best we've heard in a long time. Will you be in town next Friday? You can pick whatever songs out you want to sing."

"Aww, thank you," Jude replied. "Maybe, if my husband takes me out for dinner again."

"David laughed. "Come on wife, it's time to get you home and yes I will take you out for dinner."

21

David stoked the fire, while Jude poured extra brandy over their ice cream. When she handed David his desert she asked him, "Can we go dancing tomorrow night?"

He accepted his bowl and smiled. "As long as you don't ask me to do any dancing."

"David Wayne," she said and sat down next to him. "I have to tell you I am having the time of my life. I shouldn't tell you this, but when I lived in the city I rarely left my apartment. I was too scared. I literally ordered everything. Between my groceries and dinner orders I alone kept DoorDash and Grubhub in business." She took a spoonful of her ice cream and moaned. This is so good. Then she laughed when she told him her doorman used to set all of her Amazon packages in her apartment for her. One time he opened the box that read, cold pack and put the protein shakes in my fridge."

David watched Jude devour her ice cream, when she licked her spoon he asked her if she wanted another bowl. She cleared her throat and said she was full. When she set her bowl on the coffee table and leaned back on the couch smiling, David made a vow to always protect her. "I promise to keep you safe. I would move a mountain for you and I would be lost without you."

Jude sat up and moved closer to him, then she rested her head on his lap. "I hope our love grows every day." She took his hand in hers and held it to her chest. "I walked to my literary agent's apartment once and I couldn't believe what I saw. A man was screaming at the top of his lungs and three cops were just standing there letting it all happen. From that day forward I hailed a taxi."

When she yawned he suggested they go to bed. "I'm tired too," he said and grabbed their bowls.

Jude took the bowls from him and said she would wash them and meet him in the bedroom. "I want to get a drink of water and take two aspirins." She entered the bedroom and she stripped down to her tank top and panties. When she tossed her bra onto the chase lounge, David held up a warm bottle of message lotion. He used his finger to call her over to the bed. Then he began to rub her entire body. From her neck to her feet.

When he sniffed her hair she laughed. "Did you just smell my hair?"

"I did," he replied. Not even five minutes later, he laughed when he heard her snore. "Well, that worked. Good night, my love. I'll see you in the morning.

Around two a.m. they woke to the sound of thunder and lightning. Jude rolled over closer and David held her in his arms the entire night. When they woke the rain was pounding the windows and the sound of lightning cracked so loud, David jumped. "I'll skip jogging this morning," he said and they both laughed.

Jude stretched out her arms, kicked off the blanket and asked if he wanted to join her. "Do you want to do yoga with me?" She climbed out of the bed and headed for the bathroom, but when she saw the lightning coming in through the window, she ran back under the covers. "That was scary."

David held his hand out for her and said he would love to join her. "I'll let you teach me yoga if you let me teach you how to make ice cream."

"Deal," she said and looked over at the window. "Do you think it's safe?'

David got up, walked over to her side of the bed and walked behind her to the bathroom. "I'll wait out here for you."

"David, we're going to be married. I think you can come in. okay, no stay there," she laughingly said and sat on the toilet. When she started to wash her hands she told him, "I can see us sharing a bathroom, you shaving while I shower."

David stepped in the bathroom and stood in front of the toilet. When he started to pee, he laughed. "I had to go an hour ago."

Jude kissed the back of his shoulder and said, "I've seen it before, it's not a big deal." Then she ran out to the kitchen. She made the coffee, set four slices of toast in the toaster and suggested they go up to the cabin soon. "As much as I hate to say it, I need my laptop. Can we go to the cabin tomorrow?"

David took their eggs out of the boiling water and replied, "I can go today, it you'd like."

"No," she quickly replied. "It's supposed to rain all day today. We'll both go tomorrow, if that's okay?"

"Tomorrow it is," he said as he set their eggs and turkey sausage on their plates.

After an hour of Jude teaching David her yoga moves, he was exhausted. "Who would have thought that was hard?" he laughed adding, "That's a harder workout than jogging down the beach."

Jude wiped the sweat off her brow. "Don't think I didn't notice you not doing the downward dog, Mister."

David smiled. "Yeah, I liked the view too much." Then he jumped up and raced her to the shower. "Last one in has to make lunch."

While Jude made lunch, David cleared an entire area for her to work upstairs in his office. "Huh, I've never seen her sitting at a desk." He logged onto Cardi's Furniture Store and purchased a chase. Then he ordered a throw blanket and neck wrap. He went to close the window, but decided to leave it open. The salty scent of ocean and the sandalwood candle sitting on the table made for a relaxing and inviting room. "She'll love it," he said and heard her laugh from the bottom step.

"Do you have a mistress up there?"

"Hell no," he shouted back at her. "You're enough for me."

"Good, because your lunch is ready your Highness." They took their lunch out on the back deck. The smell of sunscreen was everywhere.

After lunch, Jude told David she was going to soak in the tub for a while. "I need to soak my bones," she said and loaded the dishwasher.

"I'm going to give Aunt Emily a call and see if July 4th works for her."

Jude smiled graciously at him. "The day we met." Then she exhales a breath she didn't know she was holding. "I can't wait."

David went to the living room and noticed the thunder and lightning had dissipated, but the rain was still coming down pretty heavy. He dialed her number hoping she had a few minutes.

She picked up on the first ring. "Hello, darling."

He laughed knowing she had just spent time with

her friend, Geraldine. "Hello to you too. Do you have a few minutes to discuss the wedding?"

"Of course, I do."

"Great, how does the fourth of July sound?"

"The day I introduced you to Jude," she replied and smiled from the inside out. "I love it. Should I order fireworks?"

"No," David replied abruptly. "I don't think Jude is a big fan of noise."

"Great, me either. In fact, I never stick around for them to go off."

"Jude and I are giving you free reign on the menu, music and wait, let me check with Jude if she wants a traditional cake or something else."

"She can have whatever her heart desires. Just let me know. How about the guest list?"

"Definitely under fifty. We're firm on that."

"Who will be your best man? You have so many friends to choose."

"Grace, I'm going to ask Grace to stand up for me. I thought about George, Dale and Henry, but honestly, I want Grace to stand next to me."

"I love the idea," she replied. "David, perhaps Jude and I should go to lunch this week to finalize the details."

"I'll check with her in an hour and have her get back to you." He looked at the mantel and saw the picture of his aunt and he was reminded how blessed he was.

"Aunt Emily, thank you and if I haven't told this lately, I love you with all my heart. Thank you for stepping up and taking care of me. I know the sacrifices you made and I appreciate everything you have done and do for me. Especially for introducing me to the love of my life."

"I love you so much young man," she whispered and hung the phone up.

"Here, here," Jude said. "That was very nice. I second that. None of this would have been possible if not for Aunt Emily. Did you know she had Grace find me that beach house?"

David stood up. "No, I did not," he replied and held his hand out for dance. He took her in his arms, leaned over and turned the stereo on. "If I Ain't Got You" sung by Alicia Keys was playing.

When the song was over Jude had tears in her eyes. David wiped them away and whispered in her ear. "I promise to love you with all my heart, to honor your wishes and to trust you with all that I have, all that I am."

22

David kept his promise and took Jude out to dinner and then an evening of dancing at Alchemy in Providence. The music was perfect, the disc jockey offered reggae vibes from the moment they entered the club. When David heard the DJ announce the next song, "Close To You" with Maxi Priest, he stood up and held his hand out to Jude. With his right hand, he held hers over his shoulder allowing her to follow him onto the dance floor. Then he pulled her in close, put his knee between her legs, locked his hip into hers and directed the movements and the flow to the music.

Jude felt his rhythm, his tenderness and his strength. She could feel herself getting hot and when the song was over she wanted more, a lot more of him. She has never felt love like this. David's sex appeal was oozing all over her, so when the song "Satisfy My Soul" with Bob Marley started, she took his hand in hers and twirled herself in a full circle before facing him. Then she showed him her moves.

David did a slow applaud before reaching out for her to come closer. "I love you," he whispered in her ear. After two slow grooves, they were both ready for another cocktail. "This is it," David said reminding her he had to drive home. "I still have to drive us back to Point Judith, remember?"

Jude's inside were hammering. She didn't want to wait another second. She whispered in his ear, "Please don't make me wait a half hour to make love to you."

David kissed her on the lips, leaned back and said, "There's always Hotel Tahoe."

Her eyes lit up. He looked at her. "You're serious?"

Jude didn't wait, she stood up, emptied her glass and grabbed him by his hand. Then she opened the back hatch and climbed inside.

The next morning, both Jude and David smiled at each other. "You are a triple threat," he said and sat up on the edge of the bed. "You sing, dance and write. I know exactly what I am getting you for Christmas."

Jude tossed back the sheet. "You had some pretty smooth moves yourself. I saw the other women looking at you." Then she went into the bathroom and called out, "Just so you know, I was ready to round-house the redhead if she winked at you one more time."

David stood in the doorway, resting on the door jam. "I never saw anyone wink at me. Trust me, I only have eyes for you. They can wink all they want. They don't stand a chance. I have everything, I ever wanted. You make me happy." Then he pointed his finger at her. "No need to be knocking anyone out." He watched as she brushed her teeth, washed her face and thought, *I am the luckiest man alive.*

Jude gave him a kiss on the cheek and said she was going to make coffee and get ready to go up to the cabin. "I need to start writing my second book in the beach series." She brushed the back of her hand against his cheek. "You inspired an entire chapter last night."

"Hey, you said I wasn't one of your test subjects." Then he laughed and said he was going jogging. "I'll be back in forty-five minutes."

"I'll have your coffee ready," she replied and put on her bathrobe.

By the time David came back, Jude had his coffee on the table along with scrambled eggs and French toast. "I made you breakfast," she said and waved the flipper in the air. Then she winked at him and told him, "I had no idea how roomy the back of that Tahoe was." She poured his coffee, gave him a kiss and said, "Thank you for satisfying my every need."

The corners of his lips rose ever so slightly. He cleared his throat before saying, "You do a pretty good job at keeping me satisfied." Then he pulled her in closer and told her, "I promise you our honeymoon will never end. Every day of our lives will be just like this."

She pulled back and laughingly said, "So you're cooking dinner tonight?"

"Yes, up at the cabin, right?"

She clapped her hands, sat down and joined him for breakfast. "If I gain weight, you're going to regret it."

"Me?" he said and pointed his fork at her. "You made the country style breakfast."

"Yes, but your ice cream is going to be the death of my waistline."

"You could gain fifty pounds and I will still love you. No fat shaming in this house. Jude, if you like something eat it." He finished his breakfast and said he wanted to call Grace before they head up to the cabin. "I'm going to take a shower and call Grace." When he went to grab their plates, Jude stopped him.

"I can clear the table, go." When he walked away she thanked God for sending David her way. "I thought I would be single for the rest of my life." She looked around, picked up their plates and added, "I can get used to this."

David got out of the shower, dressed and called Grace. "Good morning, how are you?" he asked.

"David, I'm great and you? How's Jude?"

"She's wonderful. That's why I'm calling you. Will you be my best woman?"

"What?" she shouted. "You're getting married, oh David. Yes, when?"

"The fourth of July at Aunt Emily's."

"Wow, that quick. Okay. Yes, of course. I'm so happy for the two of you." She thought about the kids. "Are children allowed?"

"Absolutely," he replied. "So how is everyone? I miss you guys."

"We miss you too. Hudson asks about you every time he talks to Aunt Emily. Have you heard the news? Ella and Brody are expecting their first baby in November."

"That's wonderful news, please give them my love and congratulations. Okay, I guess I will see everyone in July. Please say hi to Steve and tell Hudson—"

Grace sneezed and said she had to go. "We love you too, bye David."

David set the phone down wondering if he ever told Hudson that he loved them. He did love them. When Jude walked in he stood up.

"Did you call Grace?"

"Yeah," he said and started to make the bed.

"Are you okay? Is she going to do it?"

David tossed the pillows back on the bed. "Yes, she said she was happy for us and wanted me to say congratulations." Then he sat down on the bed. "I never told him I loved him. Why?"

Jude sat down next to him. "Who?"

"Hudson." He looked at Jude. "I don't think I have

ever told anyone other than you that I loved them. I tell Aunt Emily, but—"

"It's never too late to tell someone how you feel. Did you tell Grace the children are welcome to come to the wedding?"

"Yes," he replied and tapped her on her leg. "You're right, I should let them know how I feel. I guess I never told him or got close to him because I knew one day Grace would find a man he could call dad. But I do love them. It's not like the love I have for you, but I do have feelings for all of them."

"Aww, you miss them."

"Yeah, no. Not like that. And by the way, the kids are going home right after the wedding right?"

"David," she shouted and got up. Then she teased him by saying, "Actually, I thought we would bring them on our honeymoon to give Grace a break."

He jumped up, picked her up and lay her on the bed. Then he told her they needed to book their flights and reservations. "As soon as we get to the cabin, we need to make our reservations."

"Can you do it, I really want to write down my notes and start chapter one."

David rubbed his hands together. "I'm on it," he said and walked out of the bedroom.

Jude went running after him. "Wait a minute, what are you up to?" she said as she caught up to him.

He held his hand out, palm up. "I have an idea. Trust

me, you're going to love it. It will be another first for both of us."

David drove to the cabin while Jude wrote down her ideas for her next novel. When he stopped at the gate, she closed her notebook and asked, "Would you mind if I do a little writing before lunch?"

"Not at all," he replied and drove through the open gate. "I'll work on our trip."

"Hang on, David, Aunt Emily is texting me. Jude texted her back. "Next Wednesday works for me." Then she told David, "I'm having lunch with Aunt Emily on Wednesday to go over the details for the wedding." She looked over at him. "I'm sorry, I know we just got here, but I really should meet with her."

"Don't worry about it, I'll drop you off, go to the facility and meet you back at Aunt Emily's afterwards."

"I swear, you are the best." Then she got out of the vehicle, reached in the backseat and grabbed her duffle bag.

23

Ava and Shelby arrived home Sunday night. Monday afternoon Ava noticed there was only one woman in the store, she took the opportunity to talk to Ella. "I have something to show you," Ava said as she held her cellphone up. Ella looked around the room, watching the woman closely. When she saw her put a blouse in her pocketbook.

Ella held up her hand like a stop sign. "Hang on, I have to do something," she replied and walked up to the shopper. "If you can't afford to pay for your merchandise, I could always hold everything for you until you get paid."

The woman went to run away, but Ella grabbed the straps on her pocketbook. Ella pulled the strap so hard, the woman fell to the floor. Then Ella took the blouse and a scarf out of the woman's bag. "Don't ever come I here again. Do you hear me?"

The woman snatched her bag out of Ella's grip and walked out just as Ava approached them. "What the hell was that about?"

Ella explained she had been watching the woman from the moment she walked in. "She wasn't in here two seconds and she put a scarf in her pocketbook, then she stuffed a blouse in her bag. That's when I saw her look at the door." Ella looked at Ava. "What's up?" Then she pointed to Ava's cellphone. "You started to show me something."

"Oh, yeah." Ava held her cellphone up for Ella to the look at her pictures. "Scroll to the picture of Shelby and I on the beach."

Ella told Ava how beautiful they both looked. "The beach really is your happy place," she said and then held the phone closer. "Does this mean what I think it looks like?"

Ava had tears in her eyes. "Shelby makes me happy. Don't be mad. We wanted—"

Ella hugged her. "I am so happy for you and for Shelby. Ava, oh, my goodness you are married. This deserves a celebration dinner. Let's call Grace. Wait, does she know?"

Ava could feel her cheeks getting red. "She does."

"Oh my goodness, this is so exciting. Let's all go out

for a night of celebration and dancing. Jimmy will be so happy to see all three of us. Wait until we tell him, we are all married."

"You're not mad that we eloped?"

"Noooo," she replied and used Ava's phone to call Grace. "We're all married," she screamed into the phone. "I know. Right? I just told Ava this calls for a celebration. Let's all go out for dinner at to the Stonebridge Restaurant."

"Let me check with Steve and call you right back. She looks great, doesn't she?"

Ella looked over at Ava. "Like a million bucks." Then she winked at her. "Okay, call us back. I'm texting Brody right now." Ella gave Ava's shoulders a squeeze. "As long as you are happy and healthy, I am just fine. Wow, it's amazing how a few years can make a difference." She held her finger up. "Wait." Then she ran to the bathroom to throw up.

Ava texted Shelby to let her know about going to dinner. Before Shelby could answer her back, she received a group message from Grace. "Dinner reservations tomorrow night at six. I hope it's okay, we are bringing the kids."

"Absolutely," Shelby replied and Ava laughed.

"That's my wife. Always onboard." Then she went into the bathroom to see if Ella was okay. "Does this mean you're pregnant too?"

Ella came out holding a wet paper towel under her nose. "Wait, no. I'm good. Yes, we are," she replied. "And yes you will be babysitting."

Ava clapped her hands and then gave Ella a big hug. "Are you supposed to on your feet?" She shook her head. "I don't think so. You better go in the office and I will take care of the customers."

Ella smiled at her. "I'm pregnant. Geez, I can help you and believe me if I get tired I will go home." She shook her head and coughed. "I hate vomiting."

Ava was counting on her fingers. "You're two months pregnant. I think you should sit down, I read the first trimester is the hardest on the body." She put her hand on Ella's belly. "I'm going to be an Auntie. Wait until I tell Shelby, she loves kids."

Ella raised her eyebrows forming a curve. "Are the two of you going to try to have children of your own?"

Ava laughed aloud. "Hell no, between you and Grace we'll have enough children in our lives. We already discussed it. We're good at babysitting and sending them home."

Ella echoed her laugh. "Okay, I'll make sure we always have a pick up time scheduled."

"Actually, we babysat for Grace a few weeks ago and we both had a good time. I enjoyed being with them. Maddie is a trip, she's totally into fashion, makeup and learning everything there is to know about sewing. Malichi is so good with Hudson. Holds his hand, takes him to the bathroom to wash up and reads to him. Steve did a great job raising them."

"I know Brody is going to be a great dad too. He takes such good care of me."

Ava waiting for Ella to finish her thought, but when she turned to go toward the cash register, she followed her. It wasn't until Ella stopped in front of the women's bathing suits when she said, "Brody said he wants to have six kids." Ella blinked rapidly. "I almost passed out when he told me that. I thought he was joking, but damn he's serious."

"It's your body. Tell him no," Ava said and they both turned when they heard the bell on the door chime. "I'll take care of them, "Ava said and pointed to the stool behind the cash register.

Ella picked up her cellphone and read Grace's message. She smiled when she saw Shelby's reply. Ella wrote, "I'm so excited for Ava and Shelby... for all of us!" Then she read Brody's message saying he was totally onboard with going out for dinner. *I would give you a dozen children if that's meant keeping you happy.* She put a heart emoji next to his message and a thumbs up on Grace's.

Friday evening, everyone arrived at the restaurant at the same time. When they all walked in they were met by Jimmy. Ava introduced him to Shelby. "Jimmy, I'd like to introduce you to my wife, Shelby."

Jimmy held his hand out to her. Shelby shook his

hand and said she heard he was the best bartender in all of Connecticut. "It's nice to meet you, Ava has told me wonderful things about you and I hear you make a great mock cocktail."

Jimmy smiled knowing all three of them had some pretty amazing stories to share about the cocktails they've all had under his watch. "I do," he replied and pointed toward the back deck. "Your table is ready. Enjoy and ladies."

"Yes," they all said in perfect unison.

"Congratulations."

The last time Jimmy saw them they were all single, hot and now they are all glowing, married and looking finer than ever.

Of course, Maddie sat next on the other side of Ava and the boys sat next to their father. Steve reminded them to put their napkins on their lap before asking them if they were hungry. "Are you guys' hungry?"

Hudson looked up at him and then back over at his brother, Mal. "What are you having?"

Mal held his hand out. "A hamburger. What else?" and both boys laughed.

Hudson told his father he was having a hamburger too. "And French fries."

"Okay," Steve replied and then asked Maddie what she was having. "Maddie, do you see anything you'd like to try?"

Maddie looked over at Ava and then at Grace. "Mom, what are you having?"

When Grace told her she was having the salmon, Maddie asked Ava what she was ordering. "Ewe, no. Ava, what are you having?"

Ava laughed and said she was ordering the salmon as well. "Maddie put her menu down and told her father she was getting a cheeseburger. "I'll just get a cheeseburger and a small salad, please."

During dinner, Ava received a message from her wholesaler saying the entire clothing line for the homeless was being delivered on Monday. "Wow, David is going to be so happy," Ava said and set her phone down.

"About what?" Grace asked.

"He asked me to design a line of clothes for the homeless to wear and everything is being delivered to the store in Point Judith this Monday."

Ella inhaled before saying, "Take a little honeymoon and go to Rhode Island for the weekend."

Shelby tilted her head, waiting for Ava's answer, when she didn't respond right away, she said, "I think that's a fabulous idea."

Grace set her water down. "You can stay at my house and surprise David on Monday."

Ava looked at Ella. "I am not leaving you in the store by yourself; not in your condition. No way."

Grace smiled at Ava. "Always worrying about the

next person. I'll hang out with Ella on Monday, go take care of your business."

Steve sat back in his chair, leaned over and started rubbing Grace's back worrying about her being on her feet all day. Then he noticed Maddie dancing in her chair. When he winked at her she asked him if she could go.

"Dad, can I?"

Grace looked at her. "Ella, what do you think?"

"About what?"

Grace pointed to Maddie.

"Oh. Maddie, would you like to work at the store with us on Monday?"

"Would I? Yes. Thank you. I promise I won't get in the way and I'll do whatever you tell me to do," she replied and clapped her hands under the table. Then she kissed her father and whispered, "Thank you."

They were eating their desert when Jimmy came over to the table and introduced everyone to his wife and children. Steve stood up and shook her hand. "It's nice to see you again."

"Thank you," she replied and mentioned it has been a few months since they saw each other. "We only get to see everyone at baseball games."

Steve introduced Grace and everyone else to her while the children asked if they could go out on the back terrace to discuss home runs. Steve pointed to the empty chairs for Jimmy and his wife to join them just as a round of alcohol-free anise arrived. Grace, Ava and Ella smiled at each other. They were home and once again, Jimmy was taking care of them. When the hostess set down the tray of anise cookies, Ella slapped Grace's hand to get the first cookie.

Jimmy held up his shot glass. "To our friendship, may it last a lifetime!"

24

The sunset rolled in, transforming the landscape as Ava and Shelby pack the car for their long weekend away from everyone and everything. "I'm so excited to be going back to Point Judith," Shelby says causing Ava to look perplexed as she sets their snacks on the backseat.

"I thought you liked living in Connecticut?" Ava asks and slams the door harder then she intended.

"Easy girl. I do. I love living here with you, but you have to admit the waves are much better in Point Judith."

Shelby's hair whips around from the wind. "Are you ready?" she asks before getting in the car.

Ava takes a deep breath before replying, "I suppose." And gets in the car as well. "Shelby, don't you think it's strange how just a few months can make the world of difference."

Shelby started the car and pulled out onto the main road. "What are you talking about?"

"Just a few months ago the world as we knew it disappeared. Look at us now. Married, happy and yet we're going back to where it all started."

Shelby knew Ava was worried about something. "Listen to me. I love you and nothing is going to come between us, not the ocean state or—"

Ava leaned over and kissed her on the lips. "I know that. I'm just saying our lives are so different now. All of us. Grace is about to have another child, Ella is having a baby and I fell in love with a woman."

"Who loves you more than anything in the world," she replies. "Now hand me a caramel popcorn and a bottle of water please."

Ava laughed aloud. "Yes, Admiral."

Shelby made an approving noise in the back of her throat. "You're funny. Wow, are you really going to eat all of that?'

"Yeah," Ava says as she opens the party size bag of Doritos. "When Grace, Ella and I were in high school we used to have an eating contest to see who could finish the entire bag first." Then she made a terrible face. "I used to get so sick to my stomach afterwards. Now, it doesn't bother me." Ava ate a third of the bag before putting it back in the basket.

"Are you going to call David or surprise him on Monday?"

Ava pulled back her chin and smiled. "Let's surprise him. We'll go to the store and as soon as the boxes arrive, we'll go to the living facility and have Faith call him."

"What if he's not around?" Shelby asked as she took the exit for Pawcatuck.

"What? Wait. Why would you think that? I should call him. No, I'll call Aunt Emily. She'll know where he is." Ava dialed her number. "I'll put her on speaker-phone so you can say hi."

"Hello, how is my favorite fashion designer?"

Ava smiled and raised her eyebrows for Shelby to see. "I'm great. Did you hear the news? Shelby and I got married."

"That's wonderful news. Congratulations to both of you. I miss seeing the two of you," she said as she buttoned her night top.

"Thank you, Shelby said and Ava echoed her sentiments.

"Thank you," Ava replied and then asked, "Aunt Emily, by any chance do you know if David is home?"

"I believe they are up at the cabin this weekend. Do you need him?"

"I wanted to surprise him with the clothes for the homeless on Monday. Do you think I could ask Faith to make sure he is there sometime in the afternoon?"

"I don't see why not. Do you have her cell number?"

"No," Ava replied shaking her head.

"I'll text it to you. I'm sure she will make sure David is there on time. Ava, I am so happy you found true love. Shelby is an amazing woman just like yourself. You take care of each other. Bye for now."

They both looked at each other feeling sad. "I miss her," Ava said and felt tears sting her cheeks.

"She was good to all of us," Shelby replied and turned onto East Shore Road. "Are you tired?"

Ava knew how much Shelby loved walking on the beach. "Actually, I was thinking we should go for a walk. I need to burn of half a bag of chips."

"You're the best," Shelby said and parked the car in Grace's driveway. "We'll get our bags when we get back I want to stretch my legs."

As always, Narragansett offered a tranquil escape, with the setting sun painting the sky in vivid hues and gentle waves offering a soothing soundtrack. The cool sand beneath their feet and the salty air created a sensory experience allowing them to wash away their worries, leaving them feeling refreshed and not only connected to nature but to each other. Shelby reached for Ava's hand as the last silver of sun disappeared, leaving behind a sky full of stars. "Make a wish," she says as one falls toward the water's edge.

Ava squeezes Shelby's hand. "I wished for happiness."

"Me, too." Shelby says as she pulls Ava in closer. Two men started following them down the beach. Shelby is no stranger to men at night. They think no one sees them, but they're wrong. She purposely stops walking and lets them go ahead of her. When one of the men recognizes he nudges his buddy to keep walking.

"What was that about?" Ava whispers.

"Men trying to behave badly turned wrong," Shelby says laughingly. "Let's go back. I'm tired."

"You just want to get a good night's sleep so you can go surfing tomorrow morning."

Shelby stops walking. "Hey, why don't I teach you how to surf? We have all weekend."

"Really?" Ava says and holds her hands in a prayer-like pose. "I'll text Faith in the morning and see if she can make sure David is there on Monday, in the meantime, we are going to have so much fun this weekend."

Shelby knew Ava was happy, content and drug free. Her skin was glowing, her eyes sparkled. "I'm so glad you chose to go home. Grace and Ella love having you around. I think they need you more than you need them," she said as she opened the car door to get own bag.

Ava grabbed her duffle bag and said, "You're smart, and you're kind, oh and you're loyal. I love how your faith and courage push me to be a better person. I want you to be proud of me. I want to be someone you could love." Ava closed the car door. "You make me want to be brave. I love you," she whispered. "Always and forever."

25

David and Jude lie in bed beside each other, the sheets pulled up around their necks. The act of being naked, even in front of David is too novel for Jude. She spent her entire adult life alone, thinking she was entirely comfortable living without a man and now she fears being without him. She rests on her stomach, her head propped up on the pillow, watching him. Then she feels his hand trail down her spine, the sensation both soothing and ticklish. She tries to bury her face deeper into the pillow as she stifling another laugh.

"I give up; I can't take it anymore."

David grinned, wrapped his arms around her and pulled her in snug against his body, burying his face in the nape of her neck. "Have I told you how much I love you? he asks and waits patiently.

Jude turns to look up at him. "How much?'

Minutes pass. The only sound in the room is the inhale and exhale of breath. Then his fingers walk across her skin. She tips her head up for a kiss. She whispers in his ear, "Make love to me."

David shakes his head. "Whatever visions you have in your head, I want to show then to you and make them shine," he says. "I could make love to you every day and it wouldn't be enough time spent with you. I like being close to you, holding you in my arms and yes loving you."

Jude starts to cry. Hearing David profess his love for her is more than any woman could ever want. "I wasn't expecting any of this," she admits. "I came here planning on writing a novel about people living near the beach, and instead I found everything I had ever dreamed of having in my life."

David brushes a strand of hair away from face. "I promise to always be faithful and—"

"Me, too," she says adding, "I trust you and I know how blessed I am to have such a good man by my side." She laughs as she kicks the sheet down to their feet. "Now get up and make me breakfast."

David grinned. "I thought you wanted to make love?"

"An hour ago. Now I'm hungry." She sat up and said, "I'm teasing. I'll make breakfast." Jude grabbed her rode and reminded David that she was meeting with Aunt

Emily at noon. "David," she called out over her shoulder. "Can you drop me off at Aunt Emily's at eleven? I want to take a walk down the beach in her backyard to get a better look at the house at that angle."

He walked up behind her, gave her a hug and told her he would be happy to. "I'd be happy to."

They were eating avocado toast and fresh papaya for breakfast. In the background Jude had top forty music playing. She laughed aloud every time she heard David drum his fingers on the table to the beat of the music. "Do you even know the name of the song?" she asked still laughing.

David started bobbing his head to the sound. "Apt, by ROSE and Bruno Mars, thank you." Then he grabbed their plates, kissed her on the cheek. "The DJ announced the next song." He held up his coffee cup and asked, "Would you like a second cup out on the front porch?"

Jude twerked her upper lip. "Yes, smarty pants."

David was standing with his back to her when he heard her screech. He spun around and saw her standing on the chair. Then she pointed to the floor. A frog must have gotten in the house. When the frog made its familiar croak, Jude laughed. "No, I am not kissing it." She got down as she watched David carry the frog out the back door. Jude poured their coffee and met David on out the front porch.

She sat down in the rocker and stretched out her

arms. When she leaned back and closed her eyes, David smiled at her beauty. Jude was confident, smart and she seemed happy whenever they were at the cabin. He sat down beside her. Took a sip of his coffee and told her how beautiful she was. "You're even more stunning when you are here."

"I feel so relaxed when we're here. There's something about the place that I can't put my finger on it yet."

"Huh, and all this time I thought you were a city girl." Then he chuckled adding, "Until you screamed at the top of your lungs at that poor frog."

"Hahaha, I can be tough when I have to be." She stuck her chin out and said, "Huh." Then she pointed her finger at him. "My literary agent was in the hospital, after three days, she was aching to go home, but of course they don't let you go until you go to the bathroom. When she threatened to rip the intravenous line out and check herself out if they didn't let her go home; I decided to go to the store and buy either prune or pear juice so she would finally take a poop."

David looked at her lovingly, knowingly. "You're amazing."

She gave him a curtsy. "I walked eight blocks to the nearest pharmacy in order to buy prune juice. In the rain, thank you very much."

David rested his head on the palm of his hand.

"I was walking back to the hospital when I noticed four." She held up four fingers. "Four men were sitting at a café table in front of a small bodega." Her chest rise and fall remembering how scared she was. "When they got up and started following me, I picked up my pace. Thankfully, I was only a block away from the hospital." She shook her head. "That's why I have all my vitamins delivered from the pharmacy."

"I didn't love living in the city. But then again, I didn't hate it either. I lived there out of convenience. Trust me, once I talked to my editor I was convinced I could live anywhere and still have my writing career." She turned to look away. "Being here with you is like a warm hug on a cold fall afternoon. I love everything about the cabin from the fireplace to the pool house to waking up next to you in the morning."

"I know exactly how you feel. When I open my eyes and see your face smiling up at me I think I am the luckiest guy in the world."

Jude stood up, stretched her out over her head and said she needed to do some writing before she went to Aunt Emily's. "I'm going to try to write a few chapters before we go."

David stood up and kissed her good luck. "Yeah, good luck with that. I'm going jogging, I'll let Henry know you're in the pool house." When he held the door open for her to go inside, he explained, "He'll be stacking firewood this morning. I heard him splitting logs this morning."

"Gotcha," she replied and said, "I'll make sure not to

swim naked again." She ran a few steps before adding, "I'm kidding."

At ten thirty, David and Jude both made donations to two local schools. Narragansett and South Kingstown High School in the amount of ten thousand dollars each for a student seeking a career in writing and a student looking to start their own business. "Once again Mr. Wayne you have inspired me. Man that felt good."

"Sometimes I go to meet the recipients, but mostly I go to see the look of appreciation on their faces when they are handed the check."

"We both know not everyone is college material or have the funds to go to community college."

David sealed the two envelopes and told Jude if she wanted to see the view from the ocean she had better get a move on. "We should be going if you want to take a stroll before your meeting."

"Wait, you haven't told me what you want and don't say whatever I want."

David moved toward the front door. "Whatever makes you happy?" Then he waited for her comeback, but when she smiled he changed his mind. "Actually, I do have a few requests."

"Nope, too late, you just make sure you don't leave me at the altar."

Aunt Emily kissed David hello and goodbye before walking Jude to the back patio and down the stairs to the beach. "I'll wait up here for you. We'll have lemonade with fresh raspberries on the terrace when you return."

Jude blew her a kiss. As soon as she stepped onto the sand, she removed her Keds. She spent her life inland, only ever seeing the ocean in pictures or movies. Now, she lives along the blue stretches of breathtaking sights that leave her momentarily speechless. With the ocean at her back, she looked up at Aunt Emily's gorgeous mansion. The sprawling landscape, flowers and home to one of her favorite chefs. The air was thick with salty tang of the sea, her feet sink in the sand as she moves closer to the water's edge. The rhythmic sound of waves crashing against the shore fills her ears. She imagines their guests seeing the views from the advantage point of Aunt Emily's terrace and a warm smile crosses her face. "This is it," she says to only herself. A seagull is overhead and cries a stark contrast to the soothing murmur of the waves. Jude thinks, Rhode Island is truly magical.

Aunt Emily is seated at the center of the patio table with a large binder in front of her. She waves to Jude as she steps up onto the terrace. "How was your walk?"

Jude inhales once more. "Mystical," she says and takes a seat next to Aunt Emily.

Jude was sipping her lemonade when Aunt Emily opened the folder. "I love it!" she says and points to the round dance floor with all the seats wrapping around it.

"I knew you would like it," Aunt Emily replies and

adds, "This way everyone can see the two of you and you can see all of your guests. Best of all, we get to watch the two of you dance."

Jude blushed remembering their last dance. "Oh, by the way, I heard you made David take dance lessons. Thank you for that," Jude says and then asked Aunt Emily if she could use the bathroom. When she returned she said she was happy with every detail. "I love all of your ideas." Jude handed Aunt Emily the guest list and reminded her about the casual dress code. "David will be wearing a white button down shirt and khaki pants. I'll be wearing a sundress and neither of us will be wearing shoes." She waited for Aunt Emily to respond. When she didn't she said, "It's exactly what we were wearing when we met a year ago."

"David told me. Jude I am so glad you decided to come to Rhode Island and not Montauk."

Jude thought for a minute. "How?" Then she smiled. "Aunt Emily, it's your love that makes us both happy. Thank you for loving my man the way you do."

"I knew you were perfect for him." She raised her shoulders. "I did what any fairy godmother would do." She winked and opened the next folder. "I thought we would work on this." She handed a letter to Jude to read.

Jude signed it immediately. "David will be so happy. Thank you."

Both Aunt Emily and Jude's publishers agreed to donate books to David's new library at the living facility.

"After I made the special request for books on mechanics, cooking, sewing, and music, Spotify agreed to send a few CD players along with music from every music genre."

Jude shook her head in aww. "You are even more dynamic out of the kitchen than you are in one."

From behind they heard his voice. "Are you talking about me again?"

Jude leaned back and when she did, David bent down and kissed her with an upward down kiss on the lips. Aunt Emily immediately grabbed her cellphone and captured the Spider-Man kiss perfectly.

26

Monday morning, David's cellphone rang before they even rolled out of bed. Faith was calling to make sure he didn't forget to be at the facility by two o'clock that afternoon. "Hello."

"Good morning, don't forget to be here by two. You need to sign these contracts so I can get them sent out in time for Fed Ex to pick them up at four," she said and crossed her middle fingers over her pointer fingers.

"Good morning, Faith," David replied, lifted the phone away and yawned. Then he looked at the clock. He moved the phone back down to his mouth and promised to be there. "Thanks for the reminder. I'll see you at two."

Jude rolled over and asked, "Be where?"

"I have to sign for a few contracts for Faith. I'll make coffee before I go jogging."

Jude rolled over and looked at the clock. "Wow, we overslept. No more late night movies with you anymore. I'll never find my muse at this hour." She got up and followed him to the bathroom. When he went to step in she pushed him to the side and bolted for the toilet.

Laughingly, David went down the hall to the guest bathroom. He was in the kitchen putting on his sneakers when she walked in. "Can I go jogging with you?" she asked and tilted her head to the side. "I'll write in my head."

"Of course you can. Come on, you'll love it. Yesterday, I saw a fawn lying near the security gate."

Wearing a pair of jogging shorts and a sports bra, Jude asked, "Is this okay?"

David gave her two thumbs up. "Perfect." Then he waited for her to lace up her sneakers.

David thought he was going to have to slow his pace down for her, but when she got ahead of him, he picked up his pace. They jogged past the gate house and saw Henry cleaning fish near the garden hose. Both David and Jude waved to him, but he either didn't see them or care to look up.

As soon as they got back to the cabin, Jude said she was going to take a quick shower and try to write until lunch time. "I'll go with you this afternoon if that's alright with you."

"I'd like that," he replied and kicked off his sneakers.

David had just completed thirty laps in the pool by the time Jude made her grand entrance. She was wearing a pair of black skorts with a white tank top and her Keds. Her hair was tied up in a tight bun at the base of her neck. She offered a quick curtsey before sitting down in the lounge chair and opening her laptop. David smiled up at her and pointed toward the shower. When she blew him a kiss, he pretended to catch it in the air.

When Jude lived in the city, she was more like sushi and Netflix alone in her apartment than dinner seated next to celebrities in fancy restaurants. "Huh," she says aloud and then thinks. *Maybe, I should make one of my characters a hermit?* "No way, my literary agent will know it's me."

David shakes his head before asking her, "Are you talking to yourself?"

She laughs so hard, she's bursting out into a sound that alternates between trying to respond to trying to catch her breath.

"I love your laugh, although you do sound like you are suffocating," he says and waves her off before heading for the kitchen.

Jude wiped her eyes and opened her laptop. She was able to write three full chapters before declaring she had enough for the day.

At a quarter to two, David and Jude pulled up to the

facility. "Is that Ava and Shelby?" Jude asked as David parked his Tahoe.

"I think it is," he replied.

When they turned around and waved Jude called out to them. "I thought that was you. Hi."

"Hi," Ava and Shelby hollered back in unison.

David gave both women a kiss on the cheek and asked if they wanted a tour. "We can show you around as soon as I sign some documents for Faith."

"Did someone say my name?" Faith said as she approached them. Then she waved for everyone to follow her to the storeroom. Inside, Faith had four women and four men modeling Ava's designs. "I had to really turn the air conditioner up for this surprise, she said.

David gave Ava another hug. "Wow, and those?" he asked and pointed to the other boxes.

"Shelby and I wanted to donate to Auntie Em's. So we bought two-hundred more."

Jude hugged Ava and then Shelby before telling David, "You inspire us all."

Faith smiled and told them they could take off the coats, hats and gloves. "You guys did great. Thank you so much for playing along."

"It was our pleasure," they all said and told David how grateful they were. "Mr. David, thank you for my new cane," she said and walked toward the door.

David put his hand on her shoulder as he opened

the door for her. "You're welcome and if you need anything else, please let us know."

Faith winked at the men and told them she put their favorite snacks in the game room for them. "Make sure you guys win the tournament. I'll be cheering you on from the office," she said as they walked outside.

David and Jude both thanked Faith for everything. "You amaze me," David said. "And by the way, thanks for the cane."

Faith waved her hands in the air. "Not me." Then she pointed her finger at the commercial buildings and said, "The pharmacy donated them. Along with a few wheelchairs and a first aid kit for every resident. They said they drew their inspiration from you."

When Jude teared up, so did Ava and Shelby. Faith looked at them and said, "Get used to it. He's infectious."

David and Jude walked with Ava and Shelby telling them about next month's grand opening and about their wedding. "I went to Aunt Emily's house the other day and I lost my breath just looking at the back of her house."

Ava touched David on his elbow. "Angels are singing right now."

"David Wayne, no longer a bachelor," Shelby teased. "Seriously, we're happy for both of you. It's nice when your soulmate comes along."

Jude thought about Henry living alone and thought he too should have a soulmate. "I'm going to introduce my literary agent to David's friend at our wedding. I think they would make *the* perfect couple."

"Jude, you need to stop," David said to her and laughed. "Henry is content. I told you he likes living alone."

Jude shook her head and held her thumb up to Ava and Shelby. "I got this." Then she waved David off. "Imagine if Aunt Emily didn't change my itinerary?"

They all looked at her. When Jude changed the subject to lunch, David agreed to buy them lunch at JB's On The Water in Jamestown. Everyone shared an order of sweet potato fries and the caprese salad; before ordering the fish and chips for lunch. "We're celebrating," Jude said and the waitress smiled back at her.

"The Potters Cove is amazing," adding, "It has Bacardi rum, coconut rum, dark rum, orange and pineapple juice and coconut puree with a fresh squeezed lime."

"We'll take four for dessert," Jude quickly replied and everyone laughed.

During dinner, Ava excused herself, got up and walked over to the bar.

David smiled when the women all held their hands out for a picture. Their diamond rings sparkled from the glow of the candle. "I can't believe I am getting married," Jude said and then put her hand on David's. "I am so blessed and extremely thankful to Dr. Ferris for inviting me to his Fourth of July celebration." Then she laughed out loud. "I'll bet Aunt Emily told him to invite me." She winked at David. "Remind me to thank her."

Ava inhaled a deep breath remembering David picking her up off the ground. She patted his other hand. "I am so thankful for your friendship and for Aunt Emily."

The waitress came back to the table and took away their empty plates. When she returned she set their cocktails down in front of each of them. Ava's cocktail was pinker than theirs. She held her glass up and said, "Salute. To recovery, weddings and finding everlasting love."

Shelby smiled warmly at Ava knowing she exchanged her beverage for a virgin cocktail. "To strong women everywhere."

27

Grand opening day excitement filled the air. The weather gods were kind. The temperature at ten a.m. was a cool seventy-two degrees. Faith made sure there was a seat for every person. Ceiling fans blowing overhead, also under the tent were four larger fans in each of the corners. At every table refreshments and a charcuterie board that stretched from one end to the other. No assigned seats at this event, everyone sat together and from where David was standing, he couldn't tell the doctors, pharmacist or the store merchants from the residents. Everyone was smiling, having a good time and ready to start life anew. David tapped the microphone twice to get everyone's attention. "Good morning and thank you for being here," he said.

The room erupted with clapping and cheers for him.

"No, no," he replied and waved his hand out amongst the crowd. "Today is about all of you coming together, creating a sense of community and shared joy." Then David held his hand out for Faith to join him. "Everyone knows her name, but what you don't know is... Faith was once homeless. She lived in a shed in her mother's backyard for over a year before she came to work for me. As much as her husband tried to find work, he could not and so they were left to live in a ten by ten foot shed with a newborn baby and their beloved dog."

Faith nodded her head and grinned as she looked out at the crowd. "I asked David to share my story out of fear I would become too emotional. I know what it feels like to be left out in the cold with no shelter, food or medicine." She wiped away a tear, placed her finger under her nose before saying, "We got you is a phrase you are all going to hear from now on. It's not perfect English but it is the universal language for someone finally has your back." Faith pointed to everyone. "Each and everyone one of you hold a special story inside. From Dr. Nevelle pulling himself out of poverty to becoming a number one surgeon in the country to our very own pharmacist having to go to work at the age of seven to put food on the table so his family wouldn't starve. There's no such thing as homelessness in David Wayne's world."

Everyone started clapping, most stood up and the music played "Hero," by Mariah Carey. When the song was over, Faith reminded everyone, "I welcome everyone to take a tour of the entire facility, enjoy the music, dancing and the food being offered here today." She inhaled, nodded her head at the band leader and said, "We are family."

The entire day felt special. It wasn't about any one person. It was a day to celebrate coming together, fostering a sense of community and shared joy.

28

D avid was exhausted from all the excitement and so was Jude. The grand opening at the new living facility was a huge success. The publicity they received went beyond even Aunt Emily's expectations. Jude asked one of the photographers if she was available for their wedding. David was sitting at the kitchen counter working on his laptop. He drank a shot of bourbon and announced, "Our wedding is coming up in less than a month and we still haven't hired the disc jockey."

Jude grabbed herself a beer. "Let's hire the guy from Alchemy," she laughed so hard she had to cross her legs.

"Don't choke on me," David replied and looked up from his computer. "Done and done," he added and stretched his arms out. "We are all booked for our honeymoon and your wedding gift."

Still laughing, she replied, "I get both?" Then she batted her eyebrows at him. "I'll give you a dollar if you give me a hint."

David pursed his lips. "You still owe me for the pool game."

"I do not," she protested right before she squeezed an orange slice into her beer. "Who do you think paid for the one in the game room?" Then she stumbled backwards and cocked her head to the side. When she offered a sparkle in her eye, he changed his mind and gave her a hint.

"Okay, how many chapters do you have written in your story?"

Jude offered him a questioning look. "What? Why?"

"That was a hint, Jude."

She went to walk away, but he stopped her. "Wait," he said and stood up. "How would you like to go on a writer's retreat with me at the end of July?"

Her lips curled into a smile. "With you?"

He nodded a yes. "I know about how busy we have been with the facility and thought maybe a week at Ghost Ranch would be fitting."

Jude tilted her head slightly and a broad smile crossed her face.

David reached out for her hand. "We'll go straight there after our honeymoon. I read the Austin Film Festival sponsors the event."

Jude jumped into his arms. "Are you serious?"

"Oh yeah," he whispered in her ear, leaned back and said, "I figured I would make it up to you for not bringing your laptop on our honeymoon."

She kissed his entire face before saying, "I don't care if I ever write another word. I love you so much. You make me happy. My heart is full."

"So I should cancel the festival?"

"Hell no," she replied, got down and clapped her hands. "Wait, what will you do while I am writing?"

"I'll be in New Mexico, I'm sure I'll discover something wonderful." David opened his laptop and showed Jude all the adventures offered by the ranch. Swimming, horseback riding, yoga—"

"Oh, look," Jude said and pointed to the afternoon soak at the Ojo Sante Fe Spa. "We can go together."

"No, I can go. You need to finish your story."

"Can you imagine? I can get an entire novel written. Oh David, this is so exciting. I have waited my whole life for a man like you." She offered a crimson smile. "Actually, I never looked because I didn't think men like you existed." She shook her head, held out her hands and held his hands close to her heart. "You are everything women swoon over: looks, you make me laugh, and you are the most generous man I have ever met. God, I hope I never wake up from this dream."

29

The next morning, Jude closed her laptop early and headed for the shower. She was suddenly excited to go shopping for her dress, and David's wedding gift. When she walked out to the kitchen she saw a note sitting on an empty plate. "Thanks for staying at the beach house with me for one more night. I promise you tonight we will go back up to the cabin. Enjoy your lunch. I'll see you this afternoon. Love, David."

Jude opened the fridge and grabbed the bowl. "Aww, he made me my favorite-tuna with cucumber, avocado and balsamic vinegar." She sprinkled bagel seasoning on it, took her first bite and closed her eyes. "So good." She wrote on the back of his note. "I plan on spending the rest of my life showing you my love, too." Then she drew two connecting hearts at the bottom and clipped the note on the fridge.

Knowing David would only be gone a short while, Jude set out to buy her wedding dress. Unlike most brides, she was content shopping by herself, making her own decisions and feeling good about her choices. Hotter than expected she tied her hair up in a high ponytail and headed straight for the boutique. Ava told Jude about a few summer dresses she sent over to the store for her to consider.

Jude didn't take long to find the perfect dress. She fell in love with the crew neck, no sleeve midi dress. "Perfect," she said standing in front of the mirror. Jude chose the pale gray with ivory hydrangeas embroidered on it. It felt so good against her skin she didn't want to take it off. The woman suggested she wear it home. "Oh, no," Jude replied. "This is for my special day."

Down the street Jude noticed another shop had a sidewalk sale going on. She didn't have to go inside. Right there on the first table she saw a beautiful pair of Bohemian flat sandals with rhinestones that matched her dress perfectly. "I'll take these," she said the young man standing behind the cash register. Then Jude headed over to the photo shop to see if they could fill her request.

As soon as she walked in she knew they could. Jude pointed to the map of Point Judith hanging on the wall.

"Can you write this in calligraphy for me?" she handled the woman her note.

The note had David and Jude written at the top with the words Our Story underneath. Next Jude explained where the three hearts were to go. The first heart was to go on the beach at Dr. Ferris' home with the words: where we met. Then at David's beach house where he proposed those words to read: she said yes. "The last heart needs to go up here," Jude said and pointed where the cabin is. "home sweet home."

"I love it," the clerk replied and then asked when she needed it. "When would you like to pick it up? I can have it done by Monday."

Jude thought about what David said about going up to the cabin when he got home. She didn't want him to drive her to pick up his own gift so she asked if it could be delivered to Aunt Emily's in Watch Hill.

"Westerly, of course," she replied

"Thank you so much," Jude replied and handed the woman her debit card.

Jude stopped by Ferry Wharf Fish Market for some smoked trout and seafood salad. "You know what," she said the gentleman waiting on her. "That cod looks amazing. Can I have two pieces?"

When he told her the total, she laughed aloud. "I'm sorry. I feel like celebrating. Can I get a dozen oysters too?"

He pointed his finger at her. "You have a great laugh. Let me grab you those oysters." Then he pointed toward her ring and said, "He's a very lucky guy."

"Aww, thank you," she replied and accepted her bag. Outside the temperature was even hotter than when she first left the house. *As much as I want strawberry ice cream, I better get home before my fish spoils.*

Jude turned the corner down Sand Hill Cove and noticed a black SUV had pulled up alongside of her. The vehicle was moving slower than she was walking. Thinking someone was lost, she looked at the vehicle, but couldn't see the driver threw the tinted windows. Before she knew it, she felt a large hand come down on her shoulder. She gasped right before he put his other hand over her mouth. Her bags dropped to the ground.

Jude woke in a room she had never seen before. She was lying on a twin mattress. She sat up, looked up and noticed there was only one window at the top of what appeared to be a ten foot wall made of cinder blocks. She got up and saw a disgusting toilet and sink. Still trying to gain her composure and figure out what was happening she looked around the room and cried for David. The window was so small a cat couldn't escape. On the other side of the big wooden door, she could hear men talking. She checked her body for assault. Thankfully, her clothes were still intact, her ponytail was a mess but she was okay for the moment.

Jude moved closer to the door and tried to listen to what they were saying. Then the door opened and a man dressed completely in black, wearing a matching full-face hat and mask told her to sit in the corner. Jude crawled to the nearest corner, hugged her legs to her chest and forced herself to look up at him. He stared at her for a solid ten seconds before asking her if she was thirsty or hungry. Jude shook her head, no. He squinted his eyes at her before saying, "Stay here." When he closed the door behind him, Jude cried knowing she was kidnapped.

A half-hour later, a different man entered the room. He was twice the size of the first guy. Jude tried to make herself as small as she could. His stance was one of a Secret Service agent. He grunted and nodded as he set a plastic bottle of water and what appeared to be a deli sandwich wrapped in white paper down on the floor. Jude forced herself to look up and up to see his face. She clicked her tongue when they made eye contact. He shrugged inwardly. His shirt was so tight, he was one sneeze away from bursting out of it. Jude's eyebrows come together as she tried to remember if she had ever seen him before. His piercing blue eyes, demeanor and his stance. "That's all you're getting for tonight." His deep voice knocked her back to reality. As soon as he closed the door, she got up and put her ear to the door trying to remember where she heard that voice. She listened intently. Fear came over her the moment she heard someone say the word ransom.

"So, this is about money," she whispered and slid down the door.

30

D avid pulled up to the house expecting to find Jude home. When he walked into the kitchen and read her note he smiled. Then he ordered a pizza and a salad to be delivered to the cabin later that night. He texted Henry to let him know about the delivery and their return. "What can I say, she loves the place."

Henry texted him back. "Bro, she loves you. I'm happy for you. I'll stack more firewood, turn the pool temp back up and put the cushions back on the outdoor furniture. Y'all take frigging baths in that swimming pool. You need anything else, let me know."

David laughed at his joke about Jude liking it warm. "Okay, she likes it hot." Then he called the disc jockey and asked if he would play a song at their wedding as a joke. "Yeah, we danced to it at the Alchemy once. She'll get a kick out of it. Thanks."

At four o'clock David started to get worried. He called Jude's cellphone and left a message asking her where she was and if she was okay. Then he called Aunt Emily to see if Jude was with her or if she heard from her. "No, I haven't talked to Jude since the grand opening. Do you think she had to go back to the city for something?"

David blew out a long breath before saying, "She would have told me. Maybe, she's—"

"Did you call her?"

"I did," he replied. "It went straight to voicemail."

"Oh, dear. Well, writers often turn their phones off when writing. I'll call her editor and her literary agent. If I hear anything, I will call you immediately. I'm sure she's okay. Knowing Jude, she's probably at the library."

David blew out an even longer breath. "I'll call the library and ask if they saw her."

The library was closed. David decided to take a walk down the beach to see if maybe she took a stroll. He walked past the home she once rented, past Dr. Ferris' in fact, he walked all the way to Aunt Carrie's Restaurant before turning back around. David ran up the back stairs and into the beach house. "Jude," he called out. He went into the bedroom hoping she was sleeping. She was nowhere to be found.

He called Aunt Emily again. "Did you find anything

out?" he asked and sat on the kitchen stool rubbing his temple wondering where on earth she could be.

"I'm sorry dear, neither her agent nor editor heard from Jude in a month. David, I'm getting worried. Has she ever left without telling you where she was going?"

"No," David replied. "And that's why it's upsetting me. "Where can she be?"

"I'm sure she'll be walking in the door any minute, probably holding take-out."

"You're right." He set the phone down without saying goodbye.

At midnight, David sat out on the front steps. His stomach plummeted every time he thought about where she could be. Then he remembered her swimming by herself at the cabin. Fearful, she went swimming in the ocean by herself, he combed the beach again.

Six a.m., David's heart sank deeper in his chest. He went out to the back deck, held onto the railing staring out at the ocean. He called her cellphone again, this time he hung up before it had a chance to go to voice-mail. Then he called Henry. David explained the situation. "The last time I saw her was around nine yesterday morning, she was upstairs in the office writing," he told Henry and then mentioned the note she left on the fridge.

Henry thought about Jude's note. "I'm on my way. Don't call or do anything and David... we will find her."

As soon as Henry hung the phone up with David he

called Russ Benn. Russ informed Henry of a similar case he heard about in New Jersey not too long ago. "We'll need the Admiral on this one. David is big money."

A half-hour later, Henry and Russ walked into David's beach house. Both men wearing black tactical clothing, boots and belts boasting knives, a pistol and what appeared to be their cellphones. As soon as David saw Russ, he knew what Henry suspected. David's heart sank. First, his entire body stiffened at the thought of someone taking her, then he collapsed. Both men rushed to his side. Henry grabbed a glass of cold water and handed it to David. Russ combed the room for evidence. Then pointed to the note and asked if he could take a picture of it for the Admiral.

David sat with Henry and Russ for an hour explaining his every move and every conversation with Jude. When Shelby walked in wearing crye precision G4 combat olive green pants and matching t-shirt, David was not only surprised she walked in without knocking, he was even more shocked when both Henry and Russ stood at attention. "At ease," Shelby said. Walked right up to David and hugged him. "I give you my word, I *will* bring her back to you." Then she turned her attention to Henry and Russ. "What do we know so far?"

David stood stoic. Then he asked, "Can someone please tell me what is going on?"

Henry nodded to Shelby and Russ before pointing

his finger at Shelby. "David Wayne meet Admiral Shelby Warren. Better known as the enforcer."

"Enough," Shelby said and then asked David if he had a Ring camera. "Do any of your neighbors?"

"I'm not sure," he replied.

"I'm on it," Russ said and walked out the front door.

"Wow, so you weren't kidding when you said you could defend yourself." David shook his head still feeling like he just woke up from someone else's dream. Then his cellphone rang.

Shelby picked it up and looked at the call. "It's Aunt Emily." She pointed her finger at David. "From this moment on I want you to choose your words carefully. Don't give any information away."

Henry whispered, "You're still looking." Then he waved his hands in front of himself as if to say that's it.

"David," Shelby said in a low tone. "You're alone."

David answered on the fifth ring. "Hello."

"David, for heaven's sake what took you so long? Did Jude come home last night?"

Shelby shook her head no.

David answered Aunt Emily. "No, not yet. Can I call you back? I'm right in the middle of something."

"It must be pretty darn important. Call me when you hear from her. David... I love you."

"Love you too." He hung the phone up and leaned against the wall. "What is happening?"

Shelby explained, "We can't be certain, but we think someone may have taken Jude."

"Taken?" David shouted.

When his eyes filled up Shelby put her hand on his shoulder. "Stay calm. I need you to tell me everything. I want to know when, where and how long the two of you were every second this week, month."

David spent over an hour telling them about going out to lunch, dinner, dancing, walking down the beach, him dropping her off at Aunt Emily's. "She was busy writing. I didn't want to disturb her. I only left her alone for a few hours," he cried.

Russ walked in and handed Shelby a link to one of David's neighbor's Ring camera. Then he looked at Henry and shook his head. "Maybe, we should discuss this in private."

Henry saw the look in David's eye. "No," he said and waggled his finger at Russ. "David, you okay?"

David's chest was rising and falling, but Henry knew there was no way he was going to let them do any of this without him. "I'm good," David replied and then looked at Russ. "Tell us what you know."

Russ explained, "The video shows a black Escalade speeding past the house." He shook his head before saying, "They removed the plates."

A second later, David's doorbell chimed. Shelby held her finger to her lips, pointed for Russ and Henry to stand on either side of the door, then she stood behind

David and gently pushed him toward the door. "Open it slowly," she whispered.

David opened the door and saw one of his neighbors holding a bag from Ava and Ella's boutique. "I found this outside my door yesterday. The label is from the boutique down the road. The woman said your fiancé was in there yesterday and bought the dress for your wedding."

Shelby stepped in front of David. "Would you mind telling me what your address is?"

The woman told her she lived just three doors down from David. "Great, I'll walk you home," Shelby said and stepped out onto the front porch.

The woman stopped, turned around and said, "There was another bag. That one had fish in it. I wasn't sure how long it was lying in the sun, so I tossed it."

Shelby asked if she recognized the bag. "Was it from the fish market or grocery store?"

"Oh, it was from Ferry Wharf Fish Market, they always have the freshest seafood. It's a shame I had to throw it all away."

After Shelby returned she asked David for a pad of paper and a pen. "Okay, so we know she was in your office at nine, she went to the boutique, the fish market and was probably on her way home."

"Russ, call the fish market and get a time." She looked at David, who was white as a ghost. "Did you eat anything?"

"I have to call the police," he said and went to get up.

Shelby stopped him. "If you do that, we may never get her back. Look at me. Do you trust me?"

David nodded a yes as Russ sat down at the table. "Jude was at the dress shop at one and immediately went to the fish market. Both places said she was upbeat and excited. They're both sending me their security camera footage."

"I trust you guys. That's why I called Henry." He pointed toward Shelby. "I have to admit, I am a little surprised, but yes, I totally trust you."

31

J ude took a mental note of the entire room. High ceilings, one stinking window. *Where am I?* She cried inwardly, then sighed wistfully. "I'm in a hole-in-the-wall." With the morning sun beaming in she eyes the wooden door, looks up at the window that has a slight crack in it. It smells like coffee and cigarettes everywhere. Outside the rain begins pummeling the glass. It feels like days, but she knows only a few hours have passed. She stands up, but then quickly sits back down to avoid passing out. The sandwich is still wrapped and the water is un-open, she decides to drink the water before trying to get up again.

Jude crawled over to the door and pressed her ear to the door jam, she can hear them talking. Her breathing becomes erratic, her head drops down onto her chest when she hears one of the men say, "He keeps calling her cellphone. He knows she's missing."

"Let him sweat," a deeper voice replied.

Jude cries into the palms of her hands thinking about David. Just thinking about him makes her throat go tight, she scrunched her face fearful they will kill her if he doesn't find her in time. Then she openly cries thinking about them hurting him. She sucked in a deep breath as she removes her engagement ring, hoping they never noticed it. Then she kisses it and puts it in the fifth pocket of her short.

Outside, the rain slowed to a slight drizzle, storm clouds peppering the sky and for a moment Jude wished she was back in her NYC penthouse, in her writing cave, safely tucked away from everyone and everything. She whispers, "David..."

***

David looked outside as rain continued to fall. "I can almost see her. Sitting with her knees to her chest, calling out to me." When he reared his head back and blinked away his tears, Shelby knew it was up to her to find Jude as quickly as possible. When David looked at Shelby and asked her, "Who called you?"

Shelby pointed to Russ. "He sent me a text – Code: Rhode Island. Red."

"Red?" David asked.

"Yes, let's just say it's about to get real," she replied and then told Russ and Henry she wanted a full internet sweep. "David, they won't reach out to you for at least twenty-four hours. You have to be patient. Once they make that initial call, they're mine."

David looked at her intensely. "Get?"

Henry snapped his neck to the side. "May God be with them?" Then he raised his eyebrows at David.

"I promised to protect her to the ends of the earth. How am I supposed to sit here and wait for a damn call?" He got up and started pacing the floors. A few minutes later, they heard a knock on the door. Shelby looked down at her cellphone and said, "I'll get it." Three men and one woman entered holding black hard suitcases. "Shelby held her hand out for David's cellphone. "I'll need your cellphone." She plugged his phone into a voice recorder with GPS tracking. Then she sat down at the table and explained in detail what David was to say and for how long. "They know you have money," she said and David jumped up from the table.

"Jude..." He ran his hands threw his hair as if he was pulling it out. Then he sat back down and told them about the guy at George's of Galilee. "I think he heard us talking about investing twelve million in a new living facility."

Shelby looked down at the paper. "Friday night. Russ, they have a great security system at George's go see if they have any footage of David and Jude sitting topside and get me a picture of the guy."

Henry sat down next to David. "Remember, when the phone rings, stay calm. Ask to talk to Jude. She's smart, she's a writer, her creative juices are flowing, and she'll know how to give you a hint. Any clues are good clues."

David watched as the others set up machines, laptops and a big projector screen. Russ returned holding a photo of David, Jude and the man who spoke to them. A moment later, another knock on the door, this time Russ opened the door. It was David's neighbor at the end of the cul-de-sac. "I saw this on my Ring video and thought you could use it."

Russ shook his hand. "Thank you, please wait here for one minute. When he said wait here, Henry immediately went upstairs and out of sight. David wondered if Henry was hiding for a reason. Russ led the man to the kitchen and handed his cellphone to Shelby to download the video.

"Thank you, this is great," she said and handed him back his cellphone.

David stood up and shook his hand. "Yes, thank you."

"I hope she comes home soon. We were all happy the two of you met. If anyone deserves a little happiness it's you Mr. Wayne."

"Please call me David."

"Well, I'll let you get back to finding your wife."

When he saluted Shelby, she remembered exactly whom he was.

"Commander, I'll walk you to the door. When she returned she asked Russ if he remembered him.

"Oh, yeah," Russ replied and then told Henry the coast was clear.

"When this is over, I'll be asking you a lot of questions," David said to Henry.

Shelby smiled at Henry. "Tell him."

Henry looked David in the eyes before sitting down next to him. "I assaulted my Sergeant."

"Because he was raping a female private," Shelby said.

Henry raised a shoulder as if to say oh well. "It was either leave the Navy or go to prison."

"That's when I called him and told him about your job," Russ said. "The position was perfect for Henry." Then he shook his head in discuss. "It was a shame. Henry was about to take the helm of his own vessel. He just received the title of commanding officer."

Henry put his hand on David's shoulder. "It worked out for the best. Trust me, Shelby can and will protect you from various risks, including stalking, harassment, and even kidnapping." He pointed to Shelby. "She's an expert at hostage rescue, intelligence gathering, surveillance, and reconnaissance missions. Basically, you're high profile status has caught up with you and it's our job to end it."

When her team was setup they informed her they were ready. "We're one-hundred percent ready for go-code, Admiral."

Shelby thanked them and explained to David, "Commence mission, including rescue operations." She raised one shoulder. "Go-code."

David felt tears sting his eyes. "This is serious," he said and went upstairs.

Henry held up his hands as if to say stop. "Let him go. He's searched a lifetime for her. This isn't easy for him. We know we'll get her back, now we have to show him." A few minutes later, Henry went upstairs and sat down next to David. "I'm worried about my best friend." Then Henry stood back up again. "Let's find Jude."

When they walked downstairs a pizza was on the counter, along with several cups of coffee. "I need fuel," she said and pointed to the food. "Eat something. Even a bite. You need to keep your strength up."

32

S helby's personal cellphone beeped. She read the text message. "Everyone knows. Aunt Emily called us. Any word? Anything?"

Shelby texted Ava back. "No, but we're getting close. Take care of yourself, Ella and Grace. Let them know David is holding on. Ava, between you and me... he's a wreck. I love you and I will be home soon."

Russ and Henry both held their hands up as if to say what's up. Shelby shook her head. Then David's cellphone rang. Shelby called out to him. "It's Aunt Emily. David I need the line open."

"Hey, Aunt Emily. No sign of my runaway bride yet. Listen, I want to keep the phone line open in case she calls me. I promise to call you the second she is back in my arms." Without giving his aunt the opportunity to respond, David disconnected the call. "She'll understand."

Russ sat in front of one of the computers. Henry sat in front of another. An hour later, they identified the man in the photo. "New Jersey," Russ said and then pointed to his criminal record. Before they could shield it, David stood behind Shelby and read it aloud.

"Criminal possession of a weapon, robbery, and four years at Rikers Island. Great. What the hell is he doing in Rhode Island?" David said aloud.

"Great question," Shelby replied.

"I'm on it," Russ said and spun back around. A half hour later, Russ announced, "He used to work as a mechanic."

Shelby leaned in. "He's had more jobs than I have... never mind." She waved it off. "Get me a list of every garage from here to the Connecticut line."

"Got it." Russ and Henry both worked on obtaining the list of garages.

The video David's neighbor provided from his Ring video camera came back empty handed. "No frigging plates and they scratched the vin number. Damn it!" she said and threw her empty coffee cup across the room.

Russ looked over at Henry and they both knew she was about to lose it on someone. When Shelby walked out onto the back deck, David followed her. "How much longer?" he asked.

"Any minute now. I promise."

Night fell all around them. The air outside was warm and inviting. David asked if anyone wanted another cup of coffee. They all nodded yes. "I'll help you," Russ said and shrugged his shoulders. "I too need something to do."

David was just about to pour the water into the coffee pot when his cellphone rang. Potential Spam. Shelby gave David a thumbs up. Everyone held their breath.

"Hello."

David's eyes opened wide. "Yes. Absolutely. I want to talk to Jude. No, I'm not playing games. I want to hear for myself that she is okay."

"I'll call you back in an hour. If you call the cops—"

David stopped him. "I don't need to call anyone. I'm prepared to pay you whatever you want. Just let me talk to Jude."

The call ended and everyone started to breathe again.

Henry and Russ gave Shelby two thumbs up. "They're in the Wakefield area." Then they started looking at garages in all of South Kingston.

"How do they know that?" David asked.

"Shelby showed him the radar detection on the computer screen. "Next time you talk to him, he's mine. I need you to keep him on the phone for one full minute."

David gave her a hug. When he started to cry, he

apologize for being emotional. "We have to find her," he said and wiped his eyes.

Shelby held back her tears. "I give you my word, we will find her."

"David, Shelby, we got them," Henry said. "We've located several garages and a few empty buildings all within a mile radius of the call."

David yelled, "Let's go."

"No," Shelby said. "We wait."

"Shelby," David hollered and then looked at Henry and Russ. "Guys, please. It's Jude."

"David, stop. We wait for their demand. Only then will we know they didn't move her."

"She's right," Henry said and Russ echoed his sentiments. "We need certainty."

Shelby patted the seat next to her. "As soon as they call. I promise you we will get her."

David sat beside her, put his head down on the table and took a minute for himself. "This isn't happening," he said and his cellphone rang.

"David remain cool, calm and collective. I need you to keep the caller on the line for one minute." Shelby stopped him from picking the phone up. "Demand you talk to Jude or no money."

Russ handed David his cellphone. "Yes," David said as everyone read the entire conversation on the laptop.

"Ten. Million. Dollars or you never see your girlfriend again."

"I'll give you every cent I have just don't hurt her."

"I want the money by tomorrow morning at six or—"

"Stop," David said. "I said I will give you whatever you want, but I need to talk to Jude or no deal." David's heart was beating in his ears. His breathing was erratic and he was losing control. He moved the phone up so they couldn't hear him breathing, when they hung up, David screamed, "No."

***

The door opened and Jude stood up. The man leaned against the doorframe. His eyes mischievously searching her from her feet to her head. Her eyes widened, her hands were shaking, and her mouth opened. "What?" she asked and he laughed aloud at her making her feel even more vulnerable.

"Your boyfriend wants to talk to you. You have thirty seconds and that's it." He stepped back allowing her to come closer and pointed to an even bigger man.

Part of her didn't want to talk to David. She was terrified if she heard his voice, she would lose it and wouldn't be able to tell him what he needed to know. She sucked in a breath.

Before David could set the phone down it rang. "Hello?"

"David, listen to me sweetheart. I'm okay. In spite of the ten foot cinder blocks there's a small window with a hair crack that allows the morning sun to come in, so I'm not panicking. I focus on the pharmacy."

"Alright, enough." The man snatched the phone out of her hands. "I'll text you the location. As soon as I see the money you and chatty Cathy can get on with your lives."

The man pushed Jude back away from the door and told her in a belligerent tone she didn't know when to shut up. Jude fluttered her fingers in the air and said, "Even a hermit like me has encountered a few men like you living in the city." Then she swallowed the aching knot in her throat as her eyes teared up.

First he offered a scathing look then he locked the door behind him, she slid down the wall and sobbed. It frustrated her listening to them incredulously laughing. Outside, fireflies popped in and out of her view.

The call ended with a text. The drop was exactly where the calls were coming from. "This is perfect," Shelby said and then looked at the map. She drew a circle around the building. Then asked Russ to pull the address up again.

"It's an empty warehouse," Russ said and then asked David to go over everything Jude said.

Henry held the conversation up. "I knew she would be great. Writers always are."

"Yes," Shelby said. "Okay, so we're looking for high cement walls, a small window facing the east and a pharmacy?"

David grinned for ear to ear. "No, there's four men." When he told them Jude's story, they formed a group hug.

"Don't forget the crack in the window," Russ said offering a terse nod.

Shelby reached across the table and patted David's arm. "You both did great."

33

David changed his clothes. When he walked into the kitchen wearing all black, Shelby shook her head. "I'll need you to stay here," she said and both Russ and Henry shook their heads.

"Yeah, that's not happening," Henry said. "I'll take responsibility for him."

"Henry, Jude's life is at risk. I can't allow it." She held her hand up like a stop sign. "He's a civilian. He has no training." She turned toward David. "I'm sorry." Then she dialed a number and said, "I need backup. Six. Two on the ground, two drones and two to go in."

David walked up to her and said, "I'm coming. Like it or not."

"Jesus, David. You said you trusted me."

"I do and that's why I'm coming."

At midnight Shelby's backup arrived. Everyone sat in the living room. Shelby stood in front of them explaining her game plan. "They're expecting David in six hours. We're going in at three." She continued to explain in detail every person's task and the exact placement. "I want a drone facing the exit and one on that small window facing the east. If they suspect anything at all, they'll move her, hopefully the window is big enough to cast a light."

"Shouldn't someone sit outside the building now?"

"David, don't talk. If you want to go. Just listen," Henry said and David nodded.

Shelby put her hand on his shoulder. "I know you're anxious, but if they suspect someone knows their location—"

"I'm sorry. You're right. Shelby, I can take care of myself, too." He offered a confident grin. "No more words." Then he got up and went outside and sat on the back patio. Both Henry and Russ followed him.

"She's the best. Let her do her thing. Besides, they have no idea the power you have behind you."

"Gangbusters," Russ said. "She's a badass. I wouldn't mess with her."

David told them about the handprint she left on a guy who touched her buttocks. Silence when Shelby came out onto the patio and demanded they get some rest. "We have two hours before we gear up and go. Russ, you're with Henry, David I want you to stand right behind me at all times." She swatted his shoulder. "Don't make me roundhouse you. Because if you get in my way, I will knock you out." Then she turned around and went back inside.

Russ raised his eyebrows at David. "Don't get in her way, because she will knock you out."

At two-fifteen a.m., Shelby handed David a tactical helmet and vest. Unlike the others his did not have night vision, only goggles. Precisely at three a.m., Shelby entered the building, taking two men down and putting a chokehold on another one. Russ held his gun to the fourth one, while Henry and David searched the building. David stood back, stepped to Henry's side and inhaled slowly, let go both his fear and anxiety that he had been holding so tight because, at the time, he believed she was gone and if he didn't hold it in he would have lost her forever. But then his heart thumped in his chest and his throat closed as he took in one last deep breath. The scent of Calendula flowers wafted through the door in front of him. David called out for Jude, then he closed his eyes and kicked the door as hard as he could. His foot landed perfectly on the doorknob. Henry watched Jude run into David's arms. There wasn't a dry eye amongst them.

David dropped to his knees. Jude lifted David's chin proudly. "You found me, I knew you would," she said somberly and bent down, holding him tight.

David stood up, carried Jude outside, held her face

in his hands and kissed the top of her head. "Thank you California Baby."

Jude wiped his tears and laughingly said, "I could use a shower."

34

June 5th, Grace gave birth to a baby boy. A week later, Jude and David walked into the house holding gifts and toys for the other children. Grace stood up and openly cried as David held her in his arms, then she hugged Jude. "He loves you so much." Trying to stop herself from sobbing, Grace held Jude's face in her hands. "You scared the crap out of us." She wiped her eyes. "Thank God you are safe."

"Hey," Ava said as she and Shelby entered the living room.

Steve asked the children to take their gifts outside. "" I'll call you for lunch in a few minutes." Then he winked at Maddie and told her thank you."

Maddie put her hands on Mal and Hudson's back as she escorted them outside.

"I'm so excited to be David's wife." Jude touched the

side of Grace's face. "I want your glow. You look so happy and content."

Shelby, Ava, Grace and Jude formed a group hug. Steve put his hand on David's back. "Care for something to drink?"

David laughed. "I could use a cold one."

"Did I hear someone say they had cold beer?"

"Brody," Steve said and shook his hand. "David, you remember Brody."

"Yes," David said and he too shook his hand. Then David turned to face Ella. "You look radiant. Congratulations."

Ella put her hand on her baby bump and batted her eyebrows. "We are all so blessed. Thank you and I want you to know, I prayed for Jude's safe return every day. You make a great couple." She patted his hand. "It's nice to see you happy."

"You're coming to the wedding, right?"

"We're looking forward to it," she replied and laced her arm through Brody's.

Steve walked up to the bassinet and said he was going to roll it outside so he could start cooking. "I'm going to start the barbecue chicken out on the back deck."

They were sitting at the picnic table eating lunch, laughing about good times and bad. Grace had just got done breast feeding Sea. "We've seen it all," Grace said and then got up to put the baby back in his bassinet.

Steve leaned back and lifted the mesh before kissing his son on the head. Grace too kissed him, then turned and asked if everyone was ready for dessert.

Steve announced he would go inside to grab it. "I'll get the fruit salad," he said and then reminded Grace the doctor told her to take it easy for the first week. "You're supposed to be resting."

Grace rolled her eyes and smiled. "He won't let me wash my tea cup," she said laughing.

"Grace, did you name the baby after a relative?" Jude asked.

Grace allowed a broad smile to caress her face, then she reached out and held Ella and Ava's hands. "No, I named Sea after the three people I admire the most. Steve, Ella and Ava."

"I love it," Brody said as Steve set the tray down on the table. "You're a good mentor," he said as he took the small bowls out of Steve's hand and began passing them out.

Steve called out for the kids to help themselves to some fruit salad.

"I'll get the chocolate dip," Maddie said and ran inside.

"She's such a great help to me," Grace said. "I remember how tired I was when I had Hudson."

"Hey, we offered," Ella said and Ava echoed her sentiments.

"Okay, Ella offered, but I always brought pizza."

Everyone laughed. Ella rested her head on Brody's shoulder. "I think we can handle six." She winked. "As long as we can borrow Maddie."

Maddie let out a loud cheer. "I can babysit. I know how to change a diaper and I can feed the baby, oh, I'm really good at bath time."

"You're hired," Brody said and Ella agreed.

"Dad, can I take these up to the treehouse for my brothers?"

Grace smiled warmly at her. "Of course you may," Grace said and Steve echoed her sentiments.

"Thank you, sweetheart."

Grace waited for Maddie to leave the patio before telling Ava they bought Maddie a sewing machine for Christmas. "We ordered the one you mentioned with all the accessories."

Brody nodded his head at Ella. "Christmas is going to be fun. Our baby will be here in time for all the festivities." Then he kissed her temple and said, "I love you."

"I love you too," she replied and announced she wanted to host one of the holidays at their home. "We'd like to host either Thanksgiving or Christmas Eve at our house this year."

"Ooo," Grace said aloud. "We can host Thanksgiving."

David looked at Jude just as the kids ran down from the tree fort and started playing a game of tag. He reached under the table and held her hand. When she squeezed it he thanked God for bring her back to him. He took a deep breath feeling happy for his friends. Grace found love again, Ava never appeared happier and Ella had opened her heart to love and happiness. He lifted his iced tea and said it was time to make a toast. "Here's to our beautiful new beginnings, to our newfound family; may our journey together be filled with love, laughter, and endless shared memories."

They tapped each other's glasses saying cheers.

"I love you, David Wayne and I can't wait to be your wife," Jude said aloud and stood up. "I have to use the bathroom." When Jude returned she began cleaning up. Grace started to get up, but Jude stopped her. "I got this." Then she kissed the top of Grace's head. "You are such a good momma, but I want you to listen to your husband and get some rest." What Jude didn't say was Grace was pale and it looked like she lost more weight than the baby.

When the baby cried, Ava picked him up and started singing to him. She spun around fast. "No." She pointed her finger at Ella and Grace. "We plan on being the best aunties in the world and that's it!"

Everyone laughed, watching Ava bounce Sea, singing to him and making him coo.

Grace leaned over and told Steve she was happy. "My heart is full and I have you to thank for it." Then she laughed and said she was taking her business card down.

"No, you're not," Steve said and announced he still kisses it goodnight. "Now, I kiss it goodnight and thank God for sending you back to me." Everyone noticed the tears in his eyes when he said, "You rescued me and you saved our children from not knowing what a loving mother looks like."

Jude wiped her eyes before telling David they needed to get going in order to beat the Sunday traffic on I95. "If we want to be home in two hours we better get a move on."

35

There was a crack in David's cool demeanor and a flash of something that flickered in his eyes for a second when he woke up the next day. "They didn't make you want to change your mind about having children did they?" he said with a slight chuckle.

Jude sat up, stretched her arms out, leaned over and kissed him several times before putting her finger to her lips and whispering, "Shush." Then she lie next to him and rested her head on his chest. "I was actually thinking you might need to get a vasectomy." She laughed so loud, she started gasping.

David sat her up and said, "I was thinking the same." Then he shook his head. "I'm happy for them, but that's their lives. I want to spend the rest of my life with you and I don't want to share you with anyone."

Jude cleared her throat. "I feel the same. Besides we have enough on our plates." She looked over at her nightstand, noticed the lavender scented candle and inhaled its aroma before adding, "Now that we have both calmed down, I would like to work on opening that second facility with you." She glared over at him, holding his gaze and snorted once. "I just won't talk about how much—"

"Money we have..." He began tickling her. "Because, we have enough to do whatever we want Mrs. Wayne."

"Stop, stop," she cried. "I can't breathe," she added laughing.

David and Jude lie in bed for an hour and a half talking about the parcel of land he considered buying. "Let's take a ride after breakfast," he said.

"How about after lunch?" she replied. "I have a new novel to write and man do I have a story to tell." When she offered a goofy smile, David kicked the covers to the bottom of the bed.

"I'll put the coffee on and I'll make breakfast while you gather your thoughts."

Jude allowed her gaze to linger thinking about her life and how happy she was. She actually squealed. "Let's make breakfast together," she said and sat up.

After breakfast Jude wrote for five hours. Every time David peeked in on her, she was feverishly typing away at the keyboard. In spite of what happened, David decided to hire Henry as a full-time bodyguard for Jude.

At first he wasn't going to tell her, but when he did explain to her the importance of her having one, she was thankful. He laughed when she said, "Aunt Emily says Taylor Swift has like six."

David purchased a second black Tahoe for Henry to drive her where she needed to go. He grabbed the novel he was reading and went into the billiards room. He was grateful for Henry and shocked at how excited he was to have something else to do. He was still sitting in the billiards room reading when Jude asked if he wanted lunch. "Babe, are you hungry?"

David liked being called babe. "No one has ever called me that before." He stood up, gave her a hug and said, "I like being your babe. How about I take my beautiful fiancé *out* for lunch?"

"But... Henry is mowing the lawn." Then she ran her fingers under her chin and said, "You're all the protection I need. He can go shopping with me on Friday when I pick up the wedding favors."

"Oh, he'll love that." He said and texted Henry where they were going and approximately when he should expect them back. "By the way, Jude would like for you to drive her into town on Friday."

"No problem," Henry texted him back. "Let me know if you need anything else. I'll be here."

"Thanks," David typed and then opened the door for Jude to get in.

Jude loved the roadside café. She even bought a

sandwich back for Henry. "I'm telling you they are going to fall in love with one another."

"Jude, if you can make Henry fall in love that quick, you are a romance writer." Then he asked her how old her literary agent was. "How old did you say she was?"

"Old enough to recognize a hot guy," she replied and then laughed. "I have no clue." She shrugged her shoulders. "Women don't ask those questions and besides Henry doesn't seem like the man who cares how old she is. All he cares about is... does she like to fish and the answer is yes."

"Are you sure?"

"David." She laughed again. "I made sure of it. She also told me she would like to sell her apartment in the city and move to the country. Sooo."

"Jude, you have them hitched and living at the cabin."

"Stop. My name isn't Grace, Ella, Ava or Shelby."

"What does that mean?"

"I don't need a bestie up my butt twenty-hours a day. She can live in Wakefield or some other place."

David shook his head wondering what else she had up her sleeve. Then he stopped the vehicle and pointed to the open field. "What do you think?"

Jude didn't say a word, she got out and put her hands on her hips. David got out of the Tahoe and stood behind her. "How many people can live here?" she asked before walking around.

"I'm hoping we can build about a hundred more homes," he replied.

Jude spun around to face him. "How close are we to the other facility?"

"About six miles. Why?"

"Is there a way to connect the two together?"

"Not unless you want to buy several people out of their homes." He looked at her peeking through her fingers at him. Her gaze lingered.

"I have money. A lot of money," she said, her voice, barely a whisper. "Let's give it a try."

David knew of Jude's success and yes he knew she just sold her penthouse, reached number one the New York Times bestseller list, he also knew she had a heart of gold. "You're one of a kind, Mrs. Wayne and I'm the luckiest man alive." He dialed Grace's number, put his cellphone on speaker and held the phone out for Jude to hear. "You were right again. Okay, let's give it a try."

"Yay," they heard Grace say. "Okay, I'll type up the first letter and get it out in the mail tomorrow morning. You guys are going to set the world on fire, together."

"How did you know I would suggest that?" Grace said into the phone.

"Because your heart is as big as David's," Grace said. "Okay, I'll see the two of you on the third."

"Bye Grace." When Jude's cellphone rang, David motioned toward the Tahoe. Jude followed him to the vehicle.

David started the vehicle, turned the air conditioner on and began driving back to the cabin. He smiled listening to Jude talk to her literary agent about her new novel. "Do you think so?" Jude asked and reached for David's hand. "He inspires me. Oh good, I'm glad you enjoyed reading it. Yes, as soon as we get back to the cabin I'll send you the next chapter. Bye."

Jude set her phone down and asked David if he would read the same chapter she submitted to her agent. "I would love for you to read it before I send it to my editor."

"I would be honored," he replied and turned onto Point Judith Road.

As soon as they reached the cabin David asked for her laptop. "I'll print you out a copy," Jude relied and ran to their joint office.

David followed her in, sat down in the brown leather chair and waited for her to print the eleven pages. First she poured him a brandy then she handed him the papers. David reached for her hand. Grabbing her by her elbow he slowly moved his hand down her arm. When he laced his fingers in hers, he told her he wanted her to watch him read it. David set the papers down alongside his brandy, got up and poured her one. Then he pointed to the matching sofa and told her to a minute to relax while he read.

Jude's heart was racing as she sat down. Slowly sipping, watching, waiting, she couldn't take her eyes off of David as he flipped the pages. When he teared up, she smiled knowing he was on page six. David was reading the scene where the man who secretly falls in love with a woman from afar comes face-to-face with her and has to rescue her from falling off a cliff and into his arms. His heroics opens her heart and allows her to fell loved for the first time in her life.

When David set the final page down, Jude filled their glasses and moved to his lap. "That story is my biography. No one ever loved me the way you do. I never thought I would ever find love." She took in a deep breath, gazed into his eyes and told him, "My heart has never been in love like this before. I thought a love like this only existed in fairytales, but you have given me a reason to open my heart and to live every day to the fullest. I feel like I am on a cloud. I want so much for us. You make me feel like I am the only woman in the world, like no one else exists." Tears filled her eyes. "I love you so much." She giggled a sob. "Thank you for loving me."

David picked her up and carried her to the bedroom.

36

Ju1y 4th, while her guests enjoyed a private cocktail party out on Aunt Emily's terrace, Jude stood in front of the mirror as tears trickled down her face. The one women who knew her best, her literary agent and friend of the past fifteen years wrapped her arms around Jude's shoulders knowing they were happy tears. "I feel so blessed," Jude said in the mirror, wiped her eyes, and turned to face her friend. "I am so glad I never settled." She chuckled adding, "I thought I would be single for the rest of my life."

"I'm so happy for you." She replied and handed Jude a tissue.

"He makes me happy, he loves my laugh and he is the only man to make my heart feel this way." Jude wiped her happy tears away. "I'm a writer and I could never imagine writing a love story as beautiful as this. I am overwhelmed by his love, generosity and devotion to those around him. The thought of not being with him scares me. I want to be with him for the rest of my life."

"Good, because I think it's time," she said and bent down to pick up Jude's sandals. "Are you wearing these?"

Jude smiled. "No, we didn't have shoes on when we met and we're not wearing them today."

"Is that why David is walking around barefoot?" She tilted her head. "I like the way the two of you roll." Then she kicked off her Tory Burch Capri espadrilles.

David dressed in vintage washed blue jeans, a white short-sleeve button-down shirt and bare feet as he stood next to Grace wearing a pale yellow sundress and an even bigger smile than Aunt Emily. The majestic Atlantic Ocean offered a gentle breeze along with the beautiful scent of salty air as Jude stepped onto the terrace wearing a new white halter dress, no shoes and a smile so bright she could have been a beacon of hope.

Tears filled everyone's eyes watching David and Jude as they walked toward each other. David said his vows first. "I David take you Jude to be my wife. When you need a friend, I will be your best friend. When you need rescuing, I will be first at the door. When you need care, I will be there to tend to your every need. When you want to try something new, I will be by your side to encourage you and see you to the finish line. Today, tomorrow and every day from this day forward, I will be by your side for the rest of my life because I love you."

Aunt Emily wiped away her tears watching Jude wipe away David's. They looked into each other's eyes as if no one was there. Except when David leaned in to kiss Jude, she waggled her finger at him and told him not yet. Everyone laughed, including the bride and groom.

"I Jude take you David forever and forever more because before you, I never truly believed in one true love. I know now that what we have transcends into a much deeper soul connection. In you I found a partner in life, a lover, a friend, a safe place, someone I can be my ugliest and most vulnerable self with. Thank you for sharing in all of me, for lifting me up, thank you for your patience while I work, for making me breakfast every morning." Jude swallowed the lump in her throat before adding, "Thank you for loving me."

In true wedding fashion, David and Jude kissed, held their hands high above their heads, turned and smiled at their guests, as everyone cheered.

For their first dance, David and Jude chose "Because You Loved Me" by Celine Dion. They started off slow dancing until Jude stepped back and sang, "I'm everything I am because you loved me." and everyone stood up and cheered. David kissed away Jude's tears as she did his.

And when the next song came on Jude laughed hysterically and everyone was on the dance floor dancing to The Chicken Dance.

When Jude saw Henry dancing with her literary agent she smiled up at David and told him, "This is every woman's dream come true. A fairytale wedding, a love so selfless no one can break and we are blessed to have all of these people by our side." She kissed him tenderly and said, "You make all my dreams... my reality."

"Mrs. Wayne, you are my one and only dream. I have waited a lifetime for you."

"Get a room," Shelby said and bumped her hip into Jude's. "Congratulations," she shook her head. "If ever two people belonged together it's the two of you."

"Thank you," David said and Jude echoed his sentiments. The Jude hugged both Ava and Shelby. "When she whispered in Shelby's ear, they both laughed.

Ava smiled at David as she held her hand out for a dance. David winked at her and accepted her hand. "You married one hell of a badass," he said as he spun her in a full circle.

"Not bad for a forty-two-year old, right?" Ava said smiling.

"What?" David said a little louder than he intended. "I thought she was in her late twenties."

"Nope," Ava replied and switched partners. "He's a

great dancer," Ava said to Jude and reached for Shelby's hand.

Dinner was being served and everyone started to go back to their seats until the DJ played, "Uptown Funk" by Bruno Mars and the ladies had to do their thing. Ava, Ella, Grace and Shelby started dancing around Jude. When the other women joined in the men formed a circle and cheered them on.

Everyone loved the idea of the round dance floor surrounded by the half-circle table and chairs; giving every person a view of the ocean and of the bride and groom. Jude's literary agent offered the first toast, followed by Grace, but when Aunt Emily openly sobbed happy tears for Jude and David, everyone cried. "David, oh God here it goes." She looked up before continuing. "You have been one of the sweetest blessing in my life." She fanned her eyes, as did Jude. "You're a humble person who is kind, gentle and generous. At the age of fourteen you showed me what love and devotion was. Now, you have blessed me with Jude, who has been lighting up every room ever since she came into our lives. Together, the two of you will accomplish so much. I welcome Jude to our family. Jude, you are such a blessing to David. You're a role model to women everywhere. I thank God for bringing the two of you together. He knew you both needed love. I know the two of you will focus on each other's strengths. I wish you both a life full of grace and love. May you always encourage each other, lift one another up and grow in faith. I love you both."

From that moment on Jude never left David's side and he was there for every book signing, event and celebration.

QUOTE

"Never ever mistake her silence for weakness.

Remember that sometimes the air stills before the onset of a hurricane."

~ Amani al-Khatahtbeh

May the Shelby in you roar... always and forever!

ABOUT THE AUTHOR

Judy Prescott Marshall is a multi-award-winning writer of fiction with hint of romance. She earned her certificate Write Your First Novel from Michigan State University. She is currently writing her next novel. She lives with her husband, David Wayne Marshall in Dutchess County, N.Y. Sign-up for her annual newsletter at judyprescottmarshall@aol.com

ALSO BY JUDY PRESCOTT MARSHALL

Still Crazy

The Inn in Rhode Island

The Cottage at The Inn in Rhode Island

Point Judith

Salty Brine Beach

www.ingramcontent.com/pod-product-compliance
Lightning Source LLC
Chambersburg PA
CBHW050338030726
47503CB00008B/2512